True Fa

TRUE FAITH

AKA

OUR LIFE IN THE 90'S

RICHARD TERRAIN

WITH BACKING FROM JOE BLACKMORE

Prologue

Imagine a place where decades all meet together, a sort of no-man's-land between then now and the future. I need to ask you to pay close attention to what you are about to read as they don't make sense to me. Sometimes you have to let things go. Our story starts between a no-man's-land of the 80's 90's and now where months years and days all cross each other. Heroes and superstars all live alongside each other. Confused? Let's say you will be...

Evening When the sun begins to sink behind the smoke there's a burning red glow all around Watching as the colour starts to fade and the darkness seems to rise out of the ground Walls rise and fall and now they're building tall in the city Brick England They build them up and then they knock 'em down to put up another Brick England Evening creeps beyond the terrace walls up the church steeples and the chimney-pots so high Watching The moon is lost behind black clouds and the darkness seems to crawl up to the sky Walls rise and fall and now they're building tall in the city Brick England They build them up and then they knock 'em down to put up another Brick England They build them up and then they knock 'em down to put up another Brick England Brick Lane In the rain Road closed Diversion A snake of tourists meandering under grey clouds in Brick England□

CHAPTER 1

Sometime in the 90's when it's almost dawn, there comes some music, someone plays guitars, a great rendition of Pink Floyd's "High Hopes',

The room where the music played was a tip. Despite the mess the room was furnished with antiques, heirlooms and other quality stuff, Bookcase upon bookcase. A large Victorian globe sat proudly on an old wooden table. Objects d'art and breakfast remain competed for space.

There was an old high wooden chair, long past its best days. A young man sat on it. It was clear that he isn't comfortable. He leaned forward. He is looked at his thumbs almost bored. He was high yet again. He started lighting a cigarette. He took in a puff and wondered about heart attacks and blood clots, then smoked away anyway,

The man in the chair is Baxter. Twenty -nine years old. He has what could be a college look. He has on glasses like John Lennon, like the singer from the group The Beatles used to wear. Behind the glasses is a sweet face. Seventy -five per cent good looks and the rest is worry and more worry. He knows just one plain thing that are hours to go along with the bored mood.

The awful green wallpaper of the place doesn't help his mood much, sick green with spots of yellow. He thinks about reading, maybe writing but decides on something better,

Baxter reaches for a bottle of beer. The beer is cheap stuff and makes him want to vomit but he forces himself to drink the vile stuff.

What if the storm ends?

And I don't see you

As you are now

Ever again

The perfect halo

Of gold hair and lightning

Sets you off against

The planets last dance

Just for a minute

The silver-forked sky

Lift you up like a star

That I will follow

But now it's found us

Like I have found you

I don't wanna run

Just overwhelm me

What if the storm ends?

It leaves us nothing

Except the memory

A distant echo

I won't pin down

I've walked unsettled

Rattle cage after cage

Until my blood boils

I wanna see you

As you are now

Every single day

That I am living

Painted in flames

A peeling thunder

Be the lightning in me

That strikes relentless

What if the storm ends?

And I don't see you

As you are now

Ever again

The perfect halo

Of gold hair and lightning

Sets you off against

The planets last dance

Just for a minute

The silver-forked sky

Lifts you up like a star

That I will follow

But now it's found us

Like I have found you

I don't wanna run

Just overwhelm me

A kitchen extends off the living room. And is where the stuff of nightmares exists. You see the living room doesn't have a sink. This room does and it looks like it's vomited. The unwashed and the un washable are stacked to the height of the taps. Every horizontal surface is covered in shit. There are the remain of fast food and little brown bags in which they are dispensed. There are saucepans filled with unspeakable masses. Here are empty beer and wine bottles and dead -wait for it -flowers. Roses in black water like knuckles of congealed blood. This is indeed a kitchen from hell,

Baxter walks into this unholy nightmare and stops in his tracks. He stares as though witnessing this awful sight for the first time in his life.

What is it with shops abbreviating everything? You'd think there was a law in England against using whole words: newsagents sell *cigs*, greengrocers
sell *tom's* and *pot's* (always with the apostrophe) and

apparently furniture shops have taken to purveying something called a *Mem Mat.* And what the hell is that?

The *mat* bit is obvious: it's a large, grey, wrinkled-looking mattress. But *mem?* I'm half-way home on the bus before I get it.

Memory.

I'd heard about these *memory mattresses* — they were supposed to remember your body-shape and mould themselves to it. I didn't buy it: you're not fixed when you're asleep; you're on your back or your side; you stretch out, you curl up. Only time you're fixed is when you're dead.

We could do with a new mattress, though. Ours is basically two hollows — his'n'hers, with a ridge between us. But I don't want a mattress that remembers my shape. I want to be free.

Then three weeks later I came home to find a wrinkled grey *memory mattress* propped up in our hallway.
"What's *that* doing here?" I said.

Leon looked sheepish. "Mum," he said. Grace, my mother-in-law, had a habit of splurging. When the guilt kicked in, her stuff came to us.

I fingered the outside. “But it looks brand new!” I said. “Has she even slept on it?”

“She’s had it a while. But you know how she is.” Leon gave the mattress a prod: his finger sank in as though bitten off. “And you have to admit, Leuka, ours has had it.”

I couldn’t argue with that.

So we hauled the huge flat loaf up onto our bed, covering its wrinkled surface with a sheet — and that night, to my surprise, I slept unusually well. The mattress didn’t seem to mind me wriggling: it embraced all my different positions quite happily. It felt like we understood each other.

But then I had to leave. I should have got someone else to go to that damned conference, but it was too late now; and so off I went to spend two nights on a well-used hotel mattress. On the Sunday I came home and, finding Leon still out, went for a lie-down. I stretched out in my usual position. But something was wrong: the mattress wasn’t comfortable any more. Bits of it were digging into me. I wriggled around, but if anything, it felt worse. I couldn’t fathom it: we used to understand each other so well. And as I lay looking at the ceiling, a mad notion formed in my brain. The mattress had forgotten me: and that could only mean one thing. Clearly, someone else had slept in my bed.

A cry escaped me just as the front door closed behind Leon.

"Luke?"

I can hear his footsteps thumping up the stairs. I can't speak for the lump in my throat — but when he comes in, my anger speaks for me and I cry out, "who's been sleeping in my bed?"

It's pure *Goldilocks*, and I almost laugh. If I had, it could have all ended there. He would have sat down and explained; I would have laughed and perhaps we'd have made love. It could have all turned out differently.

But it didn't.

Instead, the words keep coming; the accusations, the recriminations, the realisation — oh, horror! — that but for the *memory mattress* I might never have known; and then I hear myself say, "how long has this been going on?"

I'm into song lyrics, but I never felt less like singing. Leon's face turns grey; he makes a strange noise in the throat; then he turns and leaves. Footsteps thump down the stairs; the front door opens and slams.

Then silence.

An hour later I've made it downstairs. Miserably, understanding nothing, hating everything, I pour hot water over a teabag. My feet carry me to the living room; and as I perch on the sofa, I feel a hot flush of shame. How could I have said those things? Didn't I trust Leon? Hadn't he proved himself? After all he'd been through — his father's affairs, his mother's grief, how could I? The mug is burning my fingers: as I reach to put it down I feel a lump under my leg. It's our old blue sleeping-bag, lying there like a discarded snake-skin, and on top sits a little pink card. I open it.

Thank you so much for giving me your bed. Love Mum xx.

The person who had slept in our bed was Grace.

The front door goes. Leon's standing in the doorway.

"I'm sorry," I say, in a tiny, Baby-Bear voice.

He's calmer now. "Mum wants the mattress back again," he says. "She's not been sleeping well."

He catches my penitent eye, and looks pained.

"I'm sorry," I say, in my own voice this time. "I don't know what made me think those things."

He perches next to me on the sofa. “This is crazy,” he said, “but it’s not you — it’s that bloody mattress. It’s like it’s — I don’t know, *cursed*, or something. I hate it!”

Suddenly everything makes sense. “It’s her!” I say. “It’s your mother!”

“That’s it!” he said. “My mother’s memories have *gone into the mattress*!”

We laugh, partly because it’s so ridiculous, partly from sheer relief; and before we’ve stopped laughing we’ve started to make love.

Later we manoeuvre the mattress downstairs and prop it up in the hall. As we make up the sofa-bed, it feels like when we were first married. I can remember it so well, I’m there.

He puts an old metal kettle on the gas, on a low frame,

A hypnotic blue flame circles the kettle. For a moment it demands his attention. But this thing’s beginning to bore him also. He needs a friend talk to and there is where Alice comes in.

He makes a decision and he stubs his cigarette, scarf on, long black overcoat on, he's on his way through the kitchen door and to the landing outside, music follows.

Baxter reaches the bottom of the landing and knocks on a door, "I'm going to the café for a cup of tea. God know what's breeding in that kettle of ours, (Silence.) D'you want one? (Silence.) D'you want a cup of tea, Alice?"

From somewhere we hear a sweet young sounding female voice, "No, thank you."

Without a word Baxter goes to the front door and slams the music behind him.

From someone's window The flaming lips "Bad days' plays loudly,

Outside is a boarded up shop opposite, a very crap -looking car is parked outside a line of old dwellings. Baxter fills his lungs before heading up the street he gave rant to his thoughts, "Just think of all the people in Southampton that have to wake up to this. Another day of mayhem. Another day of losing your life savings or getting drunk to block out the pain. Or if you're like me not being able to get a girlfriend to stay with you long enough, so that they can see that you're really an okay type of guy, all right I might drink a little too much, maybe take a few happy poppers and smoke a little weed. But what do you expect, it's the 1990's everyone's at it,

Think of it this way, there are perhaps two to three million people in Southampton. And they all -mostly go to have a dump once a day. That means end to end there'd be enough shit to stretch from here to New York."

The streetlights are still on. Utterly depressing. Baxter scurries along. He's a fast walker and his legs are almost a blur, "Okay my head may be spinning at the moment and maybe I'm a little stoned. But no more that Alice gets by the afternoon. I really must have a joint when I get back, one of those head blowers, like my old friend Bob used to make, when I say used to make, is because they found him stone dead last winter, some people say he was blue in the face. What a way to go, looking like an ice cube.

I don't know how Alice does it; she never gets bad highs, just giggles. Not that you would think she would try anything like that, her coming from a posh family and all. Still everyone needs to have a good time don't they, God I think I've got a headache coming on. That's all I bloody need."

Baxter turns a corner and now they're under a bridge he carried on with his thoughts. Rain hangs like dirty pest. The area is as shabby as the weather, he smiled as he thought about Alice, "Poor Alice she seems to have as much luck in finding someone as much as I do. I can't see what the problem is, we're both happy go lucky and like a laugh. I love the way she says that we'll meet the person of our dreams sometime in the future. What future?

Everything's going to shit and I think she knows it, God I could do with a beer. I bet she's got some in her room. I must ask her when I get back. That's the only way to do it. Get tanked up before the pubs open at 11 o'clock a.m. and carry on as you mean to go on. Alice and me really are unique."

An Old Git is selling newspapers under the bridge. The Old Git wipes his nose with the back of his hand. And then proceeds to pick his nose with almost childish glee. His face glows in the in the morning light. A billboard announces that a "LOLLYPOP LADY BATTERS DRIVER TO DEATH.' Before Baxter realises it he has stopped to buy a newspaper, "Evening Echo please."

The summer sun, it blows my mind

Is falling down on all that I've ever known

Time will kiss the world goodbye

Falling down on all that I've ever known

Is all that I've ever known

A dying scream makes no sound

Calling out to all that I've ever known

Here am I, lost and found

Calling out to all

We live a dying dream

If you know what I mean

All that I've ever known

It's all that I've ever known

Catch the wheel that breaks the butterfly

I cried the rain that fills the ocean wide

I tried to talk with God to no avail

Calling Him in and out of nowhere

Said if You won't save me, please don't waste my time

All that I've ever known

All that I've ever known

It's all that I've ever known

Catch the wheel that breaks the butterfly

I cried the rain that fills the ocean wide

I tried to talk with God to no avail

Calling my name and out of nowhere

Said if You won't save me, please don't waste my time

The summer sun, it blows my mind

It's falling down on all that I've ever known

Time will kiss the world goodbye

Falling down on all that I've ever known

Is all that I've ever known

Two jumps and a week

I bet you think that's pretty clever, don't you boy

Flying on your motorcycle

Watching all the ground beneath you drop

Kill yourself for recognition

Kill yourself to never ever stop

You broke another mirror

You're turning into something you are not

Don't leave me high, don't leave me dry

Don't leave me high, don't leave me dry

Drying up in conversation

You will be the one who cannot talk

All your insides fall to pieces

You just sit there wishing you could still make love

They're the ones who'll hate you

When you think you've got the world all sussed out

They're the once who'll spit at you

You'll be the one screaming out

Don't leave me high, don't leave me dry

Don't leave me high, don't leave me dry

It's the best thing that you ever had,

The best thing you ever, ever had

It's the best thing that you ever had,

The best thing you have had is gone away

Don't leave me high, don't leave me dry

Don't leave me high, don't leave me dry

Don't leave me high,

Don't leave me high, don't leave me dry

Baxter has a strange accent, a good middle -class accent that sometimes becomes posh and then almost cockney in its sound.

The Old Git gives Baxter a blank response. Baxter stoned and high, looks at the Old Git with a strange, almost forced smile. He repeats himself, “Evening News please.”

The old git looks confused, “It’s Sunday morning mate,”

CHAPTER 2

A while later, in a seedy café.

Shortly afterwards a dozen eggs billow in a massive pan. The song "When do I get to sing my way' by Sparks plays quietly in the background, Baxter sits at a table reading a newspaper, still more over powering thoughts,

"More news now as Baxter scans the newspaper. Here are murderers and muggers and photographs of tits and advertisements for chat lines and pictures of UK and U. S. pop stars and maniacal psychos and wars that never seem to end."

Wide -eyed with shock Baxter lowers his newspaper. Practically everyone else in this damp of a café is behind one. The café is a brothel of a café, seedy and unpleasant. Grease, fumes and ketchup bottles with blackened foreskins. There are some hideous faces in here. Baxter watches a young teenager eating -her fried egg sandwich which explodes in her mouth. Fascination and terror fill Baxter's soul. terror wins it and he turns away. He turns back to the newspaper and comes face to face with a headline, "I BEDDED FOUR THOUSAND MEN AND WOMEN. POP STAR TELLS ALL!' There is no escape from the awful realities from the world.

Baxter shakes his head sadly, “Is this what my whole life has become all about. Bloody mayhem and chaos. Everything’s gone to the dogs. I’m sitting in this God -for -saken place. No wonder Alice and me can’t find anyone. What are we doing here? I must be out of my mind. I must go home at once and discuss our problems in depth,”

Sip.

I ingest a single swallow and hold on. Bruno says I’ll feel the effects in a few minutes—our flasks will be nice and secure in our coat pockets. Mine’s a thin jacket on a cold night, but ink warms you up, and it tastes better with a little chill to it.

I lock my door on our way out; the city is a dangerous place these days—lately all the thugs acquired these laser box cutters to mug people like my elderly neighbour Mrs. Faust. Cauterization probably saved her from bleeding to death.

But I’m with four other dudes, a pack on the prowl with no natural predators, and now the ink’s starting to kick in. Mild euphoria, nothing major—Bruno gave me the flask, and despite what the public health people say he insists ink is fine, and if you can't trust your best friend, who can you trust?

"This is going to be a great night, Jim," Bruno says, and I couldn't have agreed more.

Slurp.

The stuff is like black honey, hard to take in large mouthfuls. Ink has power to it—every day of your life you write your story in ink. This time I can feel its power faster, like it's making the jump straight from tongue to bloodstream and bypassing digestion. My smile is huge.

Dan takes us to a club called The Hyper Dome. Everything inside is certainly hyper—flashing strobe lights and pounding music and bumping hips and bass drops. A girl in a bikini top passes us a handful of luminous sticks to wrap around our necks, wrists, hips, whatever. Bryan lingers to flirt and Dan has to drag him away, but she's good with the attention, and Bryan's good with the rejection, and I'm good with watching them—it's all good!

Glug.

The first thing I notice on the dance floor is the girl to guy ratio—so many more girls! This goes against the general rule of bars and clubs throughout the history of time, and I feel the flask in my pocket and wonder if the ink is actually changing the rules, altering the odds in the drinker's favour, contorting the very fabric of space-time itself!

There are two other guys near us, though, and Harvey steps on their toes, literally and figuratively. They are big and burly, with necks like buffaloes—football players? Harvey claims it was an accident, but he's speaking to the pair of college girls beside them. He receives a shove.

It appears the rule of numbers still exists as the five of us rush the two jocks and tackle them. The ink is pumping through my arteries now, dancing with adrenaline, thick and viscous and commanding. I'm not a fighter—I played soccer as a kid and got good at flopping—but with a dab of ink I am whatever I want to be. Right now I want to be a flurry of fists and feet.

Shouting girls attract security, and Harvey has his arm bent behind him and is steered out. His lip bleeds; he shouts profanities; we follow in their wake, glaring at the crowd that has paused mid-debauchery, though the music still thumps. Someone come for us! Someone try to take us! We dare you!

"That was some intense stuff to say, Jim," Dan says.

Had I spoken aloud?

“Well, things got heated, didn’t they?” Bruno says. “Have a sip, bro.”

Gulp.

The night air carries a thin breeze that cracks my lips, helps the blood congeal on my knuckles, seems to take my vision for a doe-see-doe as it blows by. We wander. Some of us are talking; I can’t tell who, but I can tell they’re upset by their raised voices, their tones, their shouts.

Something tells me I should find out what’s wrong. I stop and pivot, realizing I’ve roamed half a block away from my friends, who stopped to meet the two hulking silhouettes of the jocks from the club, come to finish what was started.

Harvey leads our vanguard, but apparently these two aren’t football players but heavyweight boxers—one right hook and he’s tasting sidewalk. My pack lunges; I see Bruno double over, spitting.

My legs hurl me toward them, teeth bared like a wolf, my only thought to do as much damage as possible to these intruders threatening my friends. My forehead connects with nose; my victim stumbles back. I expect him to come after me, but something steals his attention.

Three figures materialize from the shadows of low buildings—we're far from downtown now, though how we got here I couldn't say. The thugs rush us, their tattooed faces illuminated green by something in their hands.

The blow meets my side, dull at first but once I'm on the ground it becomes hot and clarifying; I see a brawl on the sidewalk; Bryan slamming into a parked car so hard its alarm goes off; a thug flailing with a box cutter so fast it spells names in the air.

One of the jocks lands an uppercut and flattens a thug. The other two turn on him. His friend with the newly broken nose rushes to help. I grab Bruno by one arm and hoist Harvey off the ground. A blink later we're all five blocks away, sprinting, running as if lions bit at our heels, turning right and flying past a gasping crowd enjoying drinks outside beneath orange heat lamps. I fumble my key out while we're still two blocks away.

Back inside, we all collapse—on couches, in chairs, on the carpet. I shrug out of my coat and examine the wound—a simple cut. Practically nothing. But my jacket is shredded, the flask inside split open, ink draining out like blood from a wound.

"Dude," Bruno pants, "save what's left."

I don't think I will.

Back home Baxter blunders upstairs. Passes the battered bathroom door on his way. As he does a woman appears. Early thirties. She is pale. Her hair is wet. Her blue eyes seem to laugh and sparkle. The face is what could be called cute -and has an air of dignity about it. So do the clothes. She wears a classy blazer. Neatly pressed trouser suit and black shoes. There is clearly class in this lady. Her name is Alice, "Morning Baxter. Listen I hate to start your day off to a bad start. But I have some rather bad and extremely worrying news,"

Her voice is a strange hybrid of someone who has lived in Oxford but thinks she's come from the North. In a way it's very enchanting. She is now speaking with deadly sincerity.

Baxter just wants to go to bed and hide, "I don't wanna hear it. I don't wanna hear anything."

Back to the living room. Nothing has changed expect that it's now filled with hot steam. Neither seems to notice and Baxter doesn't seem to remember he put the kettle on. He hotfoots it in and the pacing recommences. This time with intensity that forewarns some unseen crisis or danger.

Baxter says desperately, “My God, it’s a nightmare out there. You should have seen some of the people in the café. They were like something out of the X -Files. I tell you Alice it’s a nightmare.”

Alice just looks at Baxter in a blank way, “Never mind about that. We’ve just run out of wine and beer. What are we going to do about it?”

Baxter can’t believe what he was hearing, “I don’t care about that. You know I think I burned my brains out with all those drugs I took over the years. I don’t feel so good. I think I may have a heart attack.”

Baxter’s glasses mist with condensation. He pounds up the carpet wringing anxiety out of his newspaper, sees his reflection in a mirror. He looks at himself with horror, “Jesus Christ. I think I’ve overdone it. God you don’t think I’ve overdosed do you Alice. My eyesight’s going all funny. And my left arm has gone all weird.”

Alice sighs she’s heard all this a million times over and tries not to laugh, “Stop being so daft. Let’s have a look at that newspaper,”

She grabs the newspaper and collapses on the sofa.

Baxter is still having his panic attack, "", my hearts beating like crazy. If it goes on like this, it'll burst and I'll look like that poor sod out of that film."

Alice suddenly interested, "What film is that?"

Baxter stops having his panic attack for a moment, "You know that film where that Alien bursts out of that poor sods chest."

Alice looks thoughtful for a moment. Then she smiles, "Oh you mean the film "Alien' Yeah that was pretty good film wasn't it?"

Baxter looks at Alice as if she's gone mad, "I don't care about if the film was any good or not. You could pretend you care. I'm dying here. I'm bloody dying."

Alice snapped, "Oh stop being a drama queen. All you need is some sugar. You're not the only one with problems you know. You should see my eyes last night. They were all blood shot! A horrid sight. Now will you please stop pacing; you're making me dizzy. Go on go and get some sugar down you. You'll feel better in no time."

With that Alice starts to fight the newspaper into sharp. Baxter gathers his senses and rushes into the kitchen. He begins a frenzied search for a drinking mug. All he finds is a Mickey Mouse mug. He's transferring sugar when Alice appears through the steam.

Alice appeared in the kitchen doorway, "Listen to this. "I gave birth to an Alien Lizard Baby'"

Alice is reading from the paper with a disturbing looking grin, "I was taken abroad their mother ship and an alien probe was put up my,"

Cutting in quickly Baxter asked, "Do we have any coffee? Alice."

Confused Alice answered, "No. I didn't have time to get any. I think there's some tea bags though. You know the cheap ones that taste like crap."

Baxter goes over to a cupboard and opens it. Alice watches him, turns back to newspaper and looks up at him again. Baxter takes a tea bag and puts it into the Mickey Mouse mug.

Alice looks thoughtful for a moment and then asks quite sincerely, "If you had the chance, would you have sex with an Alien? Reading this has got me thinking about it. The way I see it they couldn't be any worse than some of the men I've slept with. I think Alien's look kinda sexy. What with those big black eyes, the oversized head? The long thin arms and such like. Only one thing gets me. They don't seem to have the bits to you know, the bits down below, so how do they, do it?"

Baxter stares at Alice, "How the hell should I know? Maybe that part's a cover up as well. Do you want a cup of tea? This is the last tea bag, but I can still reuse it to make you a cuppa."

Alice shakes her head, "No I'd rather have a beer. How long before the pub opens?"

Baxter answers like clockwork, "About an hour and a half. We could go and spend an hour in the park until then. What do you say?"

Alice smiles warmly, "Sounds great to me. You never know we might find a full beer can or two. Oh and I think you should remove that kettle from the cooker."

CHAPTER 3

A church bell tolls somewhere. Another misery Sunday. Baxter is squinting at his reflection in a puddle. Alice sits shivering on a bench like she's been there all night, "This is ridiculous you know. I don't know why we can't get a break. I mean we've both been to drama school and we did screen writing courses to boot. And look at us. Here we are sitting on a bench wondering where it all went wrong. Sometimes I think God's taking the piss."

Baxter nods seeming to agree then turns and looks shocked at Alice, "Your brother Gabriel would have a go at you, if he heard you talking like that. Him being a Priest and all."

Alice giggles, "Nuts he would. He's still a trainee Priest. I forgot to tell you he's meeting us at the pub."

Suddenly Baxter looks interested, "That's great we can talk about the horror films we like. I always found it a little odd that Gabriel liked old and new horror films."

Take the time to make some sense

Of what you want to say

And cast your words away upon the waves

And sail them home with acquiesce

On a ship of hope today

And as they land upon the shore

Tell them not to fear no more

Say it loud, and sing it proud today

And then dance if you wanna dance

Please brother take a chance

You know they're gonna go

Which way they wanna go

All we know is that we don't

Know how it's gonna be

Please brother let it be

Life on the other hand

Won't make us understand

We're all part of the masterplan

Say it loud and sing it proud today

I'm not saying right is wrong

It's up to us to make

The best of all the things

That come our way

'cause everything that's been has passed

The answer's in the looking glass

There's four and twenty million doors

On life's endless corridor

Say it loud and sing it proud today

We'll dance if they wanna dance

Please brother take a chance

You know they're gonna go

Which way they wanna go

All we know is that we don't

Know how it's gonna be

Please brother let it be

Life on the other hand

Won't make you understand

We're all part of the masterplan

We came out from the deep

To learn to love, to learn how to live

We came out from the deep

To avoid the mistakes, we made

That's why we are here

That's why we are here

That's why we are here

We came out from the deep

To help and understand but not to kill

It takes many lives till we succeed

To clear the debts of many hundred years

That's why we are here

That's why we are here

That's why we are here

That's why we are here

And that's why we are here

Alice laughs, “Why? He’s still human you know. Just because he’s training to become a Priest doesn’t mean he can’t enjoy himself does it?”

Baxter grins, “Believe me I know Gabriel can enjoy himself. I’ve seen him get drunk enough times. Isn’t he busy today, seeing its Sunday?”

Alice winks at Baxter, “He said somebody is covering for him.”

Baxter is intrigued, “Like who?”

Alice grins, “Like God.”

Baxter looks at Alice and ignores her answer, “Getting back to what you were saying before. Don’t worry one day we'll get our lucky breaks. Have you heard anything about that screenplay you sent away?"

Alice sighs sadly, "Not a thing. Most likely they threw it in the bin. Anyway let's not get down and blue. The day looks bleak enough as it is, why does it always rain. I was thinking you know what we should do?"

Baxter discouragingly, "How should I possibly know what to do? Go on then Alice; tell me what should we do?"

Alice brightly, "Get out of here. Out of Southampton for a while. Get into the countryside for a while and reenergise."

Baxter seems unsure, "I don't know. What if something goes wrong?"

Alice rolls her eyes, "What could possibly go wrong?"

Baxter sighs, "Everything goes wrong for us. It always does."

Alice is trying to encourage Baxter, "All I say is that we should think about going on holiday that's all."

Baxter pauses, thinking, "All right, we'll talk about it later."

He looks at his watch. He looks at Alice with a grin, “Well the pubs open. We’d better get along and meet him. Mustn’t keep him waiting.”

Jenny felt inside her pocket. There was a small, smooth pebble that she’d been hiding since she was tiny. A multi-dimensional creature had appeared to her and begged her to keep it safe. If she dug her fingernail into it…

But she mustn’t. She mustn’t. She had to be strong.

See, it was the self-destruct button for the universe.

And… She knew she shouldn’t use it.

She shouldn’t.

But she dug her fingernail in anyway.

And everything was over. Forever.

There are now more people about in Southampton city centre. Mainly teenagers and drunken assholes hanging around for no apparent reason. Alice hums a cheerful tune as she stops by a sad looking down -and -out. She reaches into her pocket and hands him some money. Baxter shakes his head in disbelief as he scuttles along and counts his little money.

Baxter sighs deeply and said, “All right, this is the plan. We’ll get in there and get wrecked with Gabriel. Then we’ll both have a tuna sandwich each. Then we’ll go home and drop a couple of mega poppers each. That means we’ll miss out Monday, but come out smiling on Tuesday morning. That if we don’t overdose and die of course.”

Were this a new theory of sense the answer would be the same.

Alice grins, “Sounds like a good idea,”

Baxter grumpily, “Of course it is. Nothing ever happens on Sundays or Mondays. I hate bastard Sundays and Mondays.”

The Firebird Bar is a damp of a bar. It’s filling up in direct proportions to the emptying of the churches. The bar is full of men, most of who are eyeing up Alice. She takes no notice of them. Apart from Alice there are only two other women in here and they both look like men. Faces like rotten pineapples. One has a tuft of carrot -coloured hair. Everyone here has one thing in common. They are here to get drunk. It’s a horrible place. Shit -coloured walls. Carpets like the surface of a road. The atmosphere is rank with smoke and foul language.

Alice notices a large powerfully built set -man in a black suit and overcoat. A white dog -collar noticeable. He has a shaven head but is in fact what could be called a gentle giant, but no one else knows this. When the men who are eyeing up Alice see that this giant of man knows her, they turn their eyes away from her quickly. This is Alice's brother Gabriel.

Gabriel gives both Alice and Baxter a bear hug. He orders the drinks and is served at once, "Three pints of beer. Three double shorts of rum. And I want ice in the beer."

Gabriel smiles at Alice and Baxter, and then bursts into a loud laugh, "Look at you sis. You look just like an Angel. Just like our mother did when she was alive. I hope you're looking after her Baxter."

Baxter smiles nervously, "I try my best. I even look after you Gab, when you're flat on your face."

Gabriel pats Baxter on the head in a brotherly way, "Don't worry I remember all the times you put me up when I was dead drunk. And the times you covered for me."

Alice interrupted, "So how goes the war against evil?"

Gabriel let out a laugh like that of a bear, "Well my book helps at the worst times."

Alice is puzzled, “What you mean the Bible?”

Gabriel grins a big smile, “No. My A to Z of Hammer Horror films.”

Alice stares at Gabriel in horror. Baxter isn’t listening. He’s too busy waiting for the drinks. Gabriel looks at Alice for a moment then slowly ever so slowly he breaks into a grin. Then suddenly lets out a loud lion sounding like laugh. So loud is this laugh that people in the bar stop to see what’s so funny. When they see who is laughing they just laugh nervously along. No one is going to mess with this Priest.

Alice waits until Gabriel has calmed down and the laugh has turned into a giggle, “A -of -Z of Horror indeed. You had me there for a moment. You always knew how to wind me up. “

Gabriel giggles along with her, “Sorry sis. I couldn’t resist it.”

Gabriel takes out a packet of cigarettes and offers Alice and Baxter one. They both take one. Gabriel lights his cigarette with silver lighter and then gives Alice and Baxter a light, “That’s a nice lighter. Is it real silver Gab?”

Gabriel looks shocked in a pretend way, “Of course! I carry it around in case I’m ever called out to battle a werewolf. I can have this lighter melted down into a silver bullet and use it to kill the monster. Ah, here come our drinks. Chin. Chin."

The first drinks arrive are the rums and are placed on the bar. The first three pints of lager are purely drunk out of habit. Down in one. And then we are onto the pints of beer. Enough time passes for them to get through half a glass.

Baxter looks at Gabriel and says, "Hey Gab, your sister wants to take me on a holiday. She wants to get some country air in her lungs. What do you think?"

Gabriel nods merrily a little intoxicated, "Doesn't sound like a bad idea. You should go for it. You only live once. But there's always the little matter about money."

Alice looks thoughtful. She supports herself on the bar, fiddling in the ashtray and rediscovering a thought, "I was just thinking Gab. What about what's her name?"

Alice is in a middle of a conversation that never started.

Gabriel looks at Alice puzzled and confused, "What about her?"

Alice with a sweet voice, "Why don't you give her a call?"

Gabriel asks still confused, "What for?"

Alice gestures to a phone on the wall behind Baxter's head. If Baxter wasn't so stoned and wasted, he might be able to follow the track of this complex conversation his friend is having with her brother. As it is Gabriel is having trouble keeping up with his sister, "Ask her about the house?"

Gabriel even more confused, "You want me to call what's her name and ask her about the house?"

Alice sweetly, "Yes. You could do that for your little sister couldn't you?"

Gabriel slowly catching up with the conversation, "All right. What's her number?"

Alice is at this point getting a little spaced out. As is Baxter. She thinks for a moment before replying.

Alice looks confused now, "I have no idea. I think I was very young when I last saw her."

Gabriel embarrassingly says, "Well I don't know whom you're talking about."

Alice looks at Gabriel as if he was from another planet, "Our relative. With the house in the country."

Gabriel finally realizing who she is on about, "Lady deMolay. You mean Lady deMolay."

Alice nods brightly, “That’s her! That’s the one! We could get Baxter’s car fixed up and spend a week in the country.”

Gabriel nods as well, “All right I’ll ring her. You’ll have to give us some change though. I don’t have that much change.”

Alice hands her brother some change in coins for exchange for a ten-pound note. Baxter watches all this go on with amusement. If his muscles worked, he would smile. He puts a five-pound note on the bar.

Baxter burps and says proudly, “Get a couple more in Alice. I’m going for a slash,”

Alice is putting in another order as Baxter makes his way across the bar. An enormous idiot is sitting by the lavatory door. It’s clear he’s had a few. He’s togged out in denims as if he’s trying to make himself look younger than his years. At a guess he’s in his late fortes. Obviously he thinks he’s fashion conscious. As Baxter passes, he looks up, “You gay bastard,”

Inside the gents’ lavatory Baxter starts to have another panic attack, “Why is it trouble always finds me? I don’t go looking for it. I can hardly piss straight because of fear. Here is a man with a brain the size of a pea and built like a bloody shithouse. And to top it off he's taken a dislike to me. What the hell have I done to offend him? I don't consciously offend big men like him.

This one clearly has a definite imbalance of hormone in him. If you were to get anymore masculine than him and you'd have to live up a bloody tree."

Baxter is approaching a swoon. He leans into a wall manufacturing sweat. "I LIKE BIG BOYS OR ONE'S WITH GLASSES' is etched into the plaster with dedication. His senses capsize at the implications of the threat. He catches sight of himself in a mirror, his face looking back at him, a face that wears glasses. In a panic he takes off his glasses and puts them into his pocket.

Baxter in drunken panic, "I like big boys or one's with glasses. Who the hell likes big boys with glasses? Maybe he likes big boys with glasses. Maybe he wrote this in some moment of drunken sincerity? God maybe he wants my arse, shit! I'm really in considerable danger here. I must get out of here and take Alice and Gabriel too. Otherwise he might have they're arses too. I have to get them out at once,"

Following his own advice, he zips and beats through the door.

The large idiot in the denim is still sitting outside.

The idiot looks at Baxter grumpily, "Bloody gay bastard that loves arses,"

Baxter keeps on walking and arrives at the bar. Alice looks very pleased with herself. She gives Baxter a wonderful smile, while Gabriel knocks back a pint, "You'll be glad to know that thanks to my wonderful brother here, Lady deMolay has invited us for drinks."

Baxter looks around in a panic, "Never mind that. We're getting out of here."

Alice looks at Baxter puzzled, "Why we haven't been here that long. Besides Gabriel just brought us another round."

As if to make her point Alice points to a huge round of drinks on the bar top. There has to be a good sixteen pints sitting on the top of bar.

"So I'd be buggered if I were leaving now. And you'd if a fool to miss out on my brother's good nature."

Baxter still looks around very nervously, "Listen there's a bugger over there. A bugger that like's big boys with glasses. That's why I took off my glasses. But it doesn't seem to have worked. I think he fancies me. I really think he wants our arses."

Alice takes a sip of her beer and looks thoughtful. Gabriel manipulates a mouthful of beer. Swallows it and turns.

In his panic he carries on, "Don't look, don't look. We're in danger. We gotta get out."

Gabriel is as puzzled as his sister, "What are you talking about?"

Baxter nervously carries on looking around, "I've been called a gay bastard, that likes arses."

Pissed off that somebody has called his friend a faggot, Gabriel swivels boldly on the bar, "What git called you a gay bastard that likes arses?"

The Idiot who said it has just put his full weight on his feet. And they're coming across the room. Gabriel calmly takes a swig of his beer as the Idiot comes towards him. This man might be an Idiot but he's almost as huge as Gabriel. He has red hair. Face and neck layered with stubble and bright red with drink. At the end of his arms are arguably the biggest hands in existence. Hands that Mike Tyson would be proud off.

Gabriel carries on drinking his beer the Idiot comes within inches of him. The Idiot gives Gabriel a hard evil stare, “I called him a gay bastard. And now I’m calling you a fucking gay bastard. All you fucking Priests are gay and looking to get their dicks up the other Priests arses,”

Gabriel calmly puts his drink down on the bar. While the Idiot carries on talking, “I’m going to kick the crap out of you and send you to heaven you so believe in. And then,”

, before the Idiot can finish what he saying. Gabriel kicks him in the nuts. The Idiot lets out an odd high -pitched sound from his mouth. Gabriel then proceeds to head butt the Idiot and then to as to make sure that he’s learned his lesson, Gabriel slams his fist into the Idiot’s face. The Idiot starts to cry and crawls out on his hand and knees out of the pub.

Gabriel turns and picks up his drink and starts to drink his pint, as if nothing has happened. He notices Alice and Baxter staring at him, “What’s wrong?”

Alice looks at her brother in astonishment, “Won’t you get in trouble with God for beating that man up? Not that I’m saying he didn’t have it coming.”

Gabriel looks very thoughtful for a while as he drinks his beer. Then he answers Alice, “Don’t worry sis, I won’t get in trouble with God because that man was an asshole. And God says that if an asshole is rude to a man of the cloth then he can beat the fear of God into them. Besides I can go to confession later on. And I’ll be forgiven.”

Alice looks unsure for a moment and then smiles brightly, “Oh well that’s all right then. You all right Baxter? You don’t have to worry that bullies gone now.”

Baxter bushes a bright red, “I don’t know any other way to say this. But I think I’ve crapped and wet myself at the same time.”

Alice and Gabriel just stare at him and Alice is the first to answer, “Oh dear,”

Gabriel takes a step back, “I was beginning to wonder what that smell was.”

Alice does the same and pointed towards the lavatories, “You best go to the little boys’ room and get rid of your Y - fronts and clean yourself up. Make sure you have a good clean though, otherwise the smell might hang around you all week.”

Baxter bright red mumbled, “As always you are right Alice. There is one thing you got wrong though.”

Alice looks at Baxter and wondered, “And what would that be?”

Baxter just mumbles, “I wear boxer shorts not Y -fronts.”

Gabriel sighs, “That’s great to know. Now will you please go and clean yourself up. That smells killing me.”

Baxter goes off to rest room in a hurry.

After they left the bar they start walking down the road when suddenly a small cute looking dog came walking towards the three friends. The dog walked up to the poster and lifts it’s head to take in the poster, it doesn’t seem to too impressed. As if to make its views know it corks its hind leg up and urinates in front of the poster. It looks up at the poster again with bright eyes. Still it looks unimpressed. It barks loudly as if that might help to the poster to do something.

When this fails it lifts its hind leg again and begins to crap over the pavement. Baxter and Alice and Gabriel come into view, they sidestep the dog as it does its thing. Alice glances up at the poster as they pass it, then looks down at the dog having a poo, “Says a lot about what people have to do around Southampton.”

The three friends are sitting around a table having all -day breakfasts at a place called Mike”s cafe. Gabriel is eating his huge plate of food like there’s no tomorrow. Alice and Baxter seem a little un at ease with having to eat their breakfast. Baxter toys with his food for a while and lifts his folk to his mouth. He takes a mouthful and it’s clear from his expression that the food isn’t up to much. Alice looks down at her plate and lets out a sigh. She turns to Baxter, “What do you think these red bits are Baxter?”

He looks at her shrugging his shoulders, “I think it’s meant to be bacon.”

Alice looks down at her plate again and mumbled, “It doesn’t look like bacon to me.”

Alice dares to take a mouthful and pulled a face like a child eating something new, “And it doesn’t taste like bacon neither. What about these little grey things, what are they supposed to be do you think?”

Baxter looks from his plate where he was poking around with his fork at Alice you just decided it wasn’t bacon, “I think they're meant to be mushrooms. But don't hold me to that. I've heard stories about this place."

Alice picks up a piece of something from her plate, a brown something. She looks at the piece of food stunk to her folk intently. Almost as if to make sure it's not alive when Baxter mumbles, "I heard that a lot of cat's and dogs have gone missing around this area."

Alice who is about to eat the piece of food stuck on her fork, changes her mind and puts the folk down beside her plate. Gabriel looks up from his food, "Don't you want that?"

He points at her plate when Alice shakes her head, "No. I'm not really that hungry."

Gabriel like a little schoolboy getting sweets for lunch, "Do you mind if I have it? Be a shame to waste it wouldn't it."

Alice smiles sweetly him and pushes the plate towards him, "No of course not. Help yourself."

Baxter sees a chance to get rid of his food as well, "You can have mine if you like. I've got a bit of a bellyache. Shame really as you brought all this lovely food for us."

Gabriel smiles at Baxter, “I’m sorry to hear that old friend. Pass it here then. I love the food in this place. It’s great isn’t it guys.”

Alice and Baxter both force smiles and nod. They watch as Gabriel transfers food from their plates to his. Soon there is what appears to be mountain of food on his plate. He begins to tuck in, thoroughly enjoying his meal while Alice started talking to Baxter, “Well Baxter if we play our cards right at my Lady deMolay’s we should have enough money to get away for a while.”

Baxter looks at Alice a little puzzled, “I thought she hadn’t seen since you were a little girl.”

Alice with a bright smile, “Yes but according to my dad she’s a bit,well eccentric and a little funny in the head. There was that time she got a carrot and,well I’d better not go into that. Some things are best left unsaid.”

Gabriel notices Baxter’s concerned and worried expression. He speaks to Baxter with a mouthful of food, “Don’t look so worried. That thing about the carrot was never proved in the end. The police dropped all the charges.”

Baxter cringes his teeth, “Really. That does make me feel better.”

It's clear from his tone that what Gabriel has said hasn't put his mind at rest. And what Alice says next doesn't help much neither, "Lady deMolay's always been what you could call a man -eater. The younger the better. Legend has it in my family that she once bedded her doctor, butler and maid all in the same day. You could say she's young at heart really."

Baxter looks at Alice a little confused, "Her maid?"

Alice with a grin, "She likes to swing both ways, if you get my meaning. From what I hear it something with maid that involved the thing with the carrot. As you can understand my family don't really like to talk about that."

Baxter starts to move around on his chair, "She won't make a move on me will she? I mean I'm sure she's great but the idea of my best friend Aunty making a pass at me makes me feel a little odd."

Alice giggles, "You are odd my dear. But that's what I like about you. Don't worry I'll keep an eye out for you. She won't get her paws on you while I'm there trust me. I'll have her wrapped around my little finger before you know it. We'll get the key to the place in the country and some money to boot."

Baxter a little more relaxed, “How much money do you think she’ll give us?”

Alice shrugs her shoulders, “Hard to say for sure. But it should be more than enough.”

Gabriel looks up suddenly as if he’s just thought of something very important, “I wonder if she would lend me ten thousand pounds.”

Alice looks at her brother with surprise, “What would you want with ten thousand pounds? Not even you can drink that much booze.”

Gabriel waves her off, “I don’t need it for booze.”

He thinks that matter over for a minute, “Well not all of it anyway. No what I really need the money for is so I could buy that prop suit of armour from that film we all saw a few years back.”

Baxter who is a little absent asks, “You mean Bram Stoker’s Dracula.”

Gabriel with an excited voice, “That’s right. I saw the body armour in that sci -fi restaurant we went to in London that time.”

Alice nods, “I remember, it was the Forbidden Planet restaurant. As I recall you got pissed and threw up all over our table there.”

Gabriel is a little embarrassed, “Yes sis I know. But we won’t bring that up for the moment. Just think you two what that armour would look like in the church.”

Baxter coming out of his thoughts looks at Gabriel, “I always thought you wanted a life -size Dalek.”

Gabriel exclaims, “Hell no!”

He stops talking in his tracks, “Whoops shouldn’t have used that term.”

He looks heavenwards and makes the sign of the cross over his chest, “I really will stop trying to curse my Lord. Listen you two can you just picture it in your minds, can you imagine a real prop from the film Bram Stoker’s Dracula. Not only would it put the life of God up people’s willies it would also look great. It would look fantastic in my church.”

Baxter insists, “But you said you always wanted a Dalek, you said you could also use it as a dustbin. I remember you saying that. He did say that didn’t he Alice, at our Christmas party years ago.”

Alice interrupts before they start fighting, “You did you know Gabriel. I remember it clearly because you got drunk and went outside and put a dustbin over yourself and started to act like a Dalek. You were shouting things like “You will obey’ and “I may have a sucker for an arm, but I’m all machine’ things like that.”

Gabriel brushes a bright red remembering the night now, “Okay so maybe I did say I wanted a Dalek. But you can’t have a flipping Dalek in a church. So I’ve changed my mind, I want the prop body armour from Dracula. It would look cool.”

Baxter back in his thoughts says loudly, “Would you wear the armour about in church, you know make believe you’re a vampire or something. You never know it might turn a few nuns’ heads. If you get my drift. Or would you wear the suit of armour before and while you did a sermon?”

Alice giggles, “Knowing my brother he probably would. He loved dressing up as his childhood heroes when he was little.”

Gabriel laughs taking another mouthful of the muck on his plate, “I’ll tell you what I would do. I’d wear the armour during when I collect money for the needy. If I didn’t think someone was giving enough, I'd wave my big sword around and scare the hell out of them."

Alice winks at her brother teasingly, "I'm pretty sure the ladies wouldn't want to see you waving your big sword around Gab,"

While they are talking a family sat down at the table behind them. At this table is a middle-aged couple with their boy , who is about seven or eight sitting. The father is drinking a cup of coffee, which he sips, although he clearly doesn't like the taste of it. His wife and child both have a glass of coke each.

The father looks at his wife and started talking, "Well have you given any thought to what we spoke about last night?"

The mother sighs, "Yes I've made up my mind. I've decided that the best thing to do is let Nancy have a girlfriend if that's what she wants. She's old enough now to know her own sexuality. So I think we should tell her that we don't mind her seeing other women, if she wants too. As long as she doesn't go around broadcasting it all over the place."

Alice, Baxter and Gabriel all stop talking among themselves as they hear this piece of the conversation behind their table. They all listen intently as the conversation goes on.

The father a little intensely, "Well I agree my dear. I think that's the best course of action. I really don't mind,"

The mother looks at her husband and sharply answers, "You bloody well did mind when she first told us. You didn't talk to her for a whole week. A whole week, you shut your own little girl out of your life when she needed you the most. How hard do you think this is for her?"

The father waves his wife off, "Shock woman! I was in shock. How do you think I feel being told by Nancy that she's gay. I just couldn't take it in."

The mother in a slightly angry tone of voice replies, "That's never stopped you from watching those films of yours. They all have women doing it."

The father defensively says, "That's something else completely. Those films don't have my daughter in them."

The little boy watches his parents when he interrupts, "Mum does Nancy like sleeping with other girls, because she likes them?"

The mother tries to shut her little boy up, “Hush child and drink your coke.”

The father remembers something and says, “Oh I almost forgot to tell you. Nancy came over this morning said a girl called Butch was moving in with her.”

The mother looks at her husband accusingly, “Why didn’t you tell me sooner?”

The father again waves his wife off, “For God’s sake I told you I forgot. What is it now? Can’t I forget little things like,erm, someone called Butch is moving into our spare room.”

The mother in deeper shock, “What do you mean our spare room,? What the hell are you talking about? Nancy doesn’t even live with us.”

The father mumbles, “Oh that something I forgot to tell you. Nancy was having some trouble keeping up with the rent in her place. So I said she could move back into the spare room, seeing that I turned her old bedroom into an office, it seemed like the right thing to do.”

The mother gets obviously angry, “My God. You said we should always talk about things like this together. Is this friend of her moving into the same room?”

The father tries to cut the conversation short but fails, "Of course dear. Let's not be coy, they are lovers after all. Anyway how bad can a girl called Butch be. It's a cute sounding name."

The mother looks at her husband in shock when she replies, "One day I really will have to sit you down, and explain a few things to you. I really can't believe you forgot to tell me any of this."

The little boy turns to his mother and says plainly, "Daddy forgot to tell you, because his brain's like very slow and stupid."

The father looks at his son angrily, "Shut up you little, shit!"

The mother gets defensive over her son, "Don't you dare talk to him that way! He's just a little boy. Besides which he's just stating a truthful fact."

The father replies grumpily, "You mother him too much. If I want to call my lad a little shit I should be able to. It's my right as a father."

The mother lets out a sigh, she has enough of this and she changes the subject, "Did Nancy ask you anything?"

The father thinks for a moment before he replies, “She asked if I thought you would be all right with the fact she’s gay. I told her you would be fine about it. So I told her there and then all she had to do was take a long hard look at us, if she ever wanted a true example of happiness.”

The mother starts to laugh loudly, so hard in fact that soon there are tears in her eyes, “A true example of happiness! Now I’ve heard it all. That’s the best joke I’ve heard in along time, well it’s best joke since we got married anyway.”

The father looks embarrassed at his wife and tries to calm her down, “Stop laughing. People will stare. I just told Nancy that we were bloody happy together you stupid cow. Anyway I told her we didn’t mind.”

The little boy yet again interrupts the conversation when asking, “Dad if Nancy can sleep with girls can I sleep with boys; there’s a really cool kid in school I like.”

The father looks in horror at what his son has said. The mother takes one look at her fella’s face and breaks into a load fit of laughter, in fact she laughs so much she falls off her chair laughing. While this is going on the father tries to make his son understand him, “No you can’t sleep with males. It’s not right and it’s not clever do you understand me boy. You just don't do that sort of thing. It's not what being a man's about. Two women together that's fine. When you're older you might even get a chance to watch them, two women I mean. But two men! That's a big no no. Two men together that all wrong and disgusting, you got that!"

The boy doesn't answer but just sips his coke.

Alice and Baxter are trying not to laugh at what they have just heard. Gabriel just stares down at his plate of food, a blank look on his face. His expression of what could be called sadness, with almost what appears to be a touch of shame and guilt. Alice is too busy trying not to laugh at the couple behind them to notice Gabriel's sudden mood changes. Baxter does notice however and looks at his friend with concern, "You okay their Gab?"

Gabriel looks up suddenly at the sound of Baxter's voice. He forces a smile and nods at Baxter, "What oh yeah I'm fine, ate a little too much I think. Listen I think I'd better get back to my job. It being Sunday and all there are bound to be lots of lost souls that need saving."

Alice smiles fondly at her brother, "Well don't be a stranger all right. You know you can come and visit our tip of a place any time you want."

Baxter tries to cheer his friend up, "You can come and just talk about things. We're quite good listeners when we're not that stoned or drunk you know."

Gabriel laughs and stands to leave, "I'll hold you two on that. I hope you both have a nice time at Lady deMolay's. Don't let her get her hands on you Baxter. You're never be the same drunk junkie again if she does."

With that Gabriel leaves the café. Alice holds her nose up as if smelling a nasty smell. She glances sideways at Baxter, "I think we should get home and tidy ourselves up before we go to my Lady deMolay's place. That means you better have a bath."

CHAPTER 4

Baxter looks at her in horror, “Have you seen the state of our bath? I’m not getting in that thing.”

Alice looks sternly at Baxter before she replies, “Well its either that or the swimming baths. Which I know you won’t use because you think the lifeguard there is after your body. Which I don’t see what the problem is, as I happen to think he’s quite sweet and that body of his. God what I could do with package he has in his swimming shorts.”

Baxter pulls a face and interrupts Alice’s dream, “Please I don’t want to hear anymore about his “package’ I’ll have the bloody bath okay.”

Alice smiles, “Good. Well if we go now we might miss the rain that was forecast.”

I'm always late but I caught you in time

To escape from the scene of the crime

Louder than cymbals, all out of rhyme

I give up 'cause I don't know the time

I can't decide won't you rescue my pride

Tell me the truth I have a picture of you

You have a picture of me

We could steal away in the night

Or catch the earliest flight

We're fallen in, so let's swim

You're out of my league

But I'm depending on you

You're all that I need

So why don't you say that it's true

You're out of my league but I'm depending on you

You're all that I need

So why can't you say that it's true

You're out of my league

Like a picture hung on a wall

Not a word to speak, lost for a cause

You could give me so many things

But without your love, all of it stinks

My only crime is the state of my mind

Hold on to you I have got a picture of you

You have a picture of me

We could steal away in the night

Or catch the very first flight

We're fallen in, so let's swim

You're out of my league

But I'm depending on you

You're all that I need

So why don't you say that it's true

You're out of my league but I'm depending on you

You're all that I need

So why can't you say that it's true

Hold on, people hold on

Hold on, people hold on

I ain't that superstitious

And life can be so vicious

Learning on your own

Can turn your heart to stone

Apocalyptic mind

My head was full of sorrow

Whispered words of logic

Things I need to learn

I feel like we are the only ones alive

I feel like we are the only ones alive

So hold on, hold on, hold on

Hold on, you know there ain't a lot of time

But I know that we can make it

You better hold on

You better hold on

'til you get some pepper spray

The water canons on the way

Fighting on your own

Can turn your heart to stone

And truth is on the march again

Wipe those tears away

Apocalyptic mind

She soothe me with her soul

I feel like we are the only ones alive

I feel like we are the only ones alive

So hold on, hold on, hold on

Hold on, you know there ain't a lot of time

But I know that we can make it

You better hold on

So hold on, hold on, hold on

You better hold on, you know there ain't a lot of time

But I know that we can make it

You better hold on

You better hold on

You better hold on

You better hold on

I feel like we are the only ones alive

I feel like we are the only ones alive

I feel like we are the only ones alive

I feel like we are the only ones alive

Well you better hold on

You better hold on, hold on

You better hold on, you know there ain't a lot of time

But I know that we can make it

You better hold on, so hold on

You better hold on, hold on

You better hold on, you know there ain't a lot of time

But I know that we can make it

'til you get some pepper spray

The water canons on the way

Apocalyptic mind

She soothe me with her soul

I feel like we are the only ones alive

Apocalyptic mind

I feel like we are the only ones alive

Jandwat knew he was going to copulate tonight. No matter what his wife said.

"If we aren't home for the latest holo-episode of Galactic Crime Investigators, there'll be no mating ritual," she said.

Jandwat rolled his eyes as he set the coordinates for Tau Ceti e. "Relax. Taking off in 5, 4, 3—" he hit the launch button early, setting off the centrifugal force stabilizer which blew enough air on Komway's head that her tentacles lost their cultivated poof and went flat. She hadn't had time to dodge it like normal.

"Zhanget," she yelled the Tau Ceti en curse meaning: you who smells with ears and hears nothing. "Do you know how much the stylist cost? That's it. No mating ritual." She crossed her four arms.

As the saucer shot above the clouds, Jandwat leveled it out.

"Aren't we going interplanetary?" Komway asked.

"I didn't come here just to scare locals. I need a smoke before we leave the atmosphere."

"Open the window. I don't like that stink. I don't know why you insist on that foul plant."

He took out papers, pulled a tobacco leaf apart and sprinkled the remnants onto the small sheet. "You know it relaxes me."

"We have substitutes."

"Says the woman who's never smoked."

She huffed and stared out the window. Jandwat finished rolling his cigarette and lit it with his purloined Zippo. When he activated the Love Connector — as he liked to call it — he knew she would come around. The pheromone optimizer never failed.

"I said, roll down the window."

Jandwat pulled back on the accelerator and set the ship to cruising speed so the air wouldn't storm through the cabin. The internal atmosphere stabilizer would take care of the rest.

He waved his hand at the window, which receded into the ship's frame. He blew a smoke ring, letting the wind from outside pull the perfect circle to pieces, then reached into the wall compartment for his Love Connector. He wanted to slip it into his pocket without drawing attention. She'd buried it in the biopit behind their hab, but he'd found it and hid it in the ship. He'd be needing it tonight.

He flipped the "on" switch and moved the Love Connector toward his pocket. The device worked best when the "subject" was exposed to the pheromone optimizing rays for prolonged periods, and they had hours to go before reaching home. It only needed to be within six feet. They'd both be in the right mood by the time they reached Tau Ceti e.

At first, Jandwat didn't notice the hot ash. Until he felt the burn. Without thinking, he started slapping his tunic, forgetting all about the Love Connector. It escaped his grasp and flew out the window. Too late, Jandwat lunged, jerking the controls in the process and sending the ship thrusting hard left.

"What're you doing?" Komway yelled as the centrifugal force stabilizer lost its battle with Newton's Third Law and she hit the wall.

He sighed, and righted the ship. Komway detached herself from the wall and tried to reform her tentacles into something resembling style.

"What was that?" she asked.

"Oh that… nothing. Just a bauble from one of my trips."

"Mmm hmmm. Definitely no mating ritual."

Jandwat frowned. The Love Connector was falling to Earth, and pheromone optimizers weren't meant for humans.

***

Jandwat drove the tiller over the tobacco field gloomily. He hated it here. He missed the adventurous, unkempt travelers of the intergalactic highway. These Earth people were… well, rubes. He never thought the Intergalactic Panel on Earth Affairs would rule how they did, but they were furious that he'd lost the pheromone optimizer.

The Love Connector had an amplified effect on humans. And the area covered by the one he'd lost was the entire United States. Unless his people wanted the country's population to soar to unsustainable levels, they needed to intervene. Nobody liked Earth. So they made Jandwat go.

He finished the last row and steered towards the house where his wife stood with her two arms crossed.

“Hi, dear,” he called as he exited the tiller.

“Don’t dear me. I’ve been cooking all morning for the Rotary bake sale. You’ve got it easy.” She said it in an irritated voice, but with a smile.

Other than a few quick trips for tobacco, Komway had never really experienced Earth. But now that they lived here, she discovered she loved it. Back home, she’d complained people were too busy and disconnected. Here, in her new body and with all her new human friends, she was content. It helped that the ladies in the small town said she had the most stylish hair. On the plus side for Jandwat, happiness had made Komway amorous. On the downside, he’d been smoking his own crop since arriving on Earth. So until recently, Jandwat wasn’t in the mood.

“I’ll help. I just need to put the compound in the sprinklers and water the crops.”

The Board had given Jandwat a sexual-dulling concoction to put in the tobacco he grew. In addition to nicotine, tar and the roughly 443 other toxins the smokers would be inhaling, they’d get a Tau Ceti en chemical that would render them uninterested in sex. It wouldn't reach all smokers, but he was farming for a major tobacco company. The Tau Ceti en scientists said it would be enough. At least until the phermone optimizer could be found and turned off.

The chemical also meant fewer children with a propensity towards addiction. Smokers wouldn't beget smokers, and eventually the smoking population would be far smaller.

"I'm so glad you are part of the solution," Komway said. "These smokers are scum."

"That's not fair. The tobacco companies lied about the addictive properties—"

"You should know," she interrupted. "You're one."

Jandwat walked over and put his arms around her. "I quit last week." He kissed her full human lips.

"Ooh, Jandwat," she said. "You know, tonight's the mating moon."

"I know, dear."

Baxter and Alice's bathroom is a psychological nightmare to cleanliness. It is in fact very unclean. At some point in the past somebody has had an epileptic fit in here with a can of green paint. There is wet rot and dry rot. A poster of the music group Radiohead clings to one of the walls.

Baxter mutters to himself, "Speed is like a dozen transatlantic flights with out getting off the plane. Times change. Sometimes you lose. Sometimes you a high in life. It makes no difference as long as you keep taking the pills,"

The room is very small. There is a lavatory at one and a bath at the other end. Baxter is sitting up in it. Pocked and shocked and attempting to shave. He wears an old woolly top rolled up just under his armpits. This obviously affords protection against the cold. A mirror is propped behind the taps. His reflection appears in it.

Baxter still muttering to himself, "But there always comes a time, when the high ends. And so begins the never-ending quest to find a higher high. Because the high that you've just had is crashing around you. And all at once those frozen hours melt through the nervous system and seep out the pores."

He rinses his shaving razor and shivers. Alice bursts in wearing nothing but her underwear. Baxter carries on trying to shave; the sight of Alice doesn't seem to have any effect on him. He's seen her like that a million times before. Alice clutches a couple of tuna sandwiches in her hands.

Brightly Alice asks, "I brought these on our way back home. 2 bloody quid for next to nothing. Knowing our luck, the tuna more likely off. I'll put yours by the sink."

Baxter looking a little sick answers, "Thanks Alice."

Alice lowers the toilet seat, not before having a look at what's down there. She doesn't appear to like what she sees. Having lowered the seat, she sits and starts to eat her tuna sandwich.

Baxter finishes shaving. He looks across at Alice who seems to be enjoying her sandwich a little too much. The sounds she makes as she eats, you would think she was making love to the sandwich.

Baxter asks Alice in a mono tone, "Could you pass me my sandwich; you're making me feel hungry."

Alice stops making her loving making to a sandwich sounds, and hands Baxter his sandwich. Baxter sniffs the tuna; it appears to be all right. He takes a small bite, tastes great. He takes out a big bite of the sandwich, and lets out a sigh of joy. Then he thinks for a moment and asks,

Baxter asks plainly, ", why are we having dinner in here?"

Alice nods eating, "Because you're in the bath silly and I'm sitting here on the toilet in my underwear. Oh and I think I saw David climbing through the downstairs window a moment before I came in here."

Baxter lets out a sigh as if this was a everyday thing, "I wonder what he wants now?"

Alice giggles, "He's more than likely feeling lonely. That's why he normally comes here. That and to get pissed and very, very stoned."

Alice makes a face and asks in a strangely cheerful way, "Do you mind if I have a pee? I'm bursting to go."

Baxter starts his sandwich and nodded a little nod, "Knock yourself out. I normally piss in front of you anyway."

While Alice goes about having her, pee, Baxter finishes his tuna sandwich. His eyes focus on the mirror in front of him. In the background we hear what could be water flowing, though of course it's not. It's Alice having her pee.

Baxter thought to himself, “So David’s here. King drunk and full-blown junkie head. If you think Alice and me are bad wait until you see David. David doesn’t really have any friends. The only people he converses with are his “clients’ and occasionally the police. To some junkies in Southampton, David is the stuff of myth. The purveyor of rare herbs and prescribed chemicals is back in our lives. Will we never be set free?”

Alice appears to be peeing for England. Outside the bathroom David waits, David is a man who has kept the “News Of The World’ in business through most of the late 1980’s and most of 1990’s. He has dedicated his adult life to drugs. And it really shows.

He is a wreck. About sixty except he just a little older than Baxter. A streak of white in his hair and he has on night - black sunglasses. Get down, punks. This man is before you were born.

Baxter walks in wrapped in a dirty towel. David is a sort of posh Cockney. At times the voice is monotone almost robotic.

David looks Baxter up and down, “You’re lookin’ very hip and cool man. Have you been away?”

Baxter shakes his head. Fills the kettle and puts it on the cooker.

David sighed a sad sigh and sniffed, "I was wondering do you and the lovely lady have any food. I've not eaten for a week. Well tell a lie I did find a burger in a bin today."

Baxter nods, "We've got a few tuna sandwiches. Here,"

The item is handed across. David examines it as he was unsure what it was. He gives it a sniffing and decides he likes it.

David asks as if in fear, "How much do you want for it?"

Baxter forces a smile, "You can have it for nothing."

Alice walks in. She seems to brighten the room as she enters. She is re -togged in a lovely black and silver dress. It's old but has quality. Possibly came from a will in her family. David looks across with curiosity.

David eyeing Alice up, "I see you're wearin' a dress."

Alice smiles, "Yes I thought I'd make an effort. Do you like it? It's not to flash is it?"

David shakes his head smiling, "No! No it's very fetching. It shows off your great legs. Can I ask, are those stockings with a G - String that you're wearing?"

Alice with a look, “Of course I’m wearing stockings with some G -Strings, it’s too bloody cold not to wear them.”

David takes a bite out of his sandwich. He eyes Alice up and down as he eats.

David says in an almost creepy way, “I must tell you, that at this moment in time, I’m getting rather odd feelings down below. Feelings that I didn’t think I’d ever have again. It really is a most odd and strange feeling. But also rather an exciting feeling as well.”

Baxter giggles, “I wouldn’t worry about it David. You’ve got a hard on that’s all. Just sit back and enjoy it.”

Alice smiles brightly, “Wow I’ve turned on David. And to think people were saying he couldn’t get it up in the pub the other day. I’m glad I was able to help. You know I’m quite fluttered.”

“I don’t suppose you would go the whole way and have hot kinky sex with me,” David asks without emotion.

Alice thinks it over and shakes her head, “I would but I have someone else in my heart at the moment.”

David looks startled, “Who would that be then Alice?”

Alice smiles sweetly, “I’m not saying. I tell that person how I feel when I’m good and really. I’ll wait for the right magic moment. Only thing is, I just hope it won’t be unrequited love.”

Baxter looks thoughtful for a moment, “Sometimes you have to go through area’s of unrequited love. You know before you find that someone who feels the same way.”

Alice smiles as if in a wonderful daydream, “Well I know whom I want to spend the rest of my life with. And if I have to wait for him or her then so be it.”

David takes one long stare at Alice’s figure then conducts an audit of an ashtray. Finds a suitable butt, “I’m sorry to say this but I can’t offer you and the lady any thing at the moment.”

Alice smiles gently looking at Baxter, “That’s all right David. We decided to lay off pot for a while. Baxter’s been getting some God-awful trips lately.”

David nods as if he’d heard this all before, “I know what he’s been going through. “Cept for personal use, I concur with you. As a mattera of fact, I’m thinking of retirin’ and goin’ inta business.”

Baxter can’t believe his ear, “Doing what?”

David face fills into a huge smile, “The Bathroom industry. Well the part that makes toilets really.”

Alice looks up from re -adjusting her stockings to ask something, “Why toilets?”

David answered, “Because my dear people will always need toilets. What’s the first thing someone does when they get up?”

Alice and Baxter think for a moment then together, “They all have a shit.”

David looks at them smiling still eating his sandwich, “That’s right everyone shits, some more than others. But in the end people will always need a good old toilet to crap in.”

In the time of chimpanzees, I was a monkey

Butane in my veins and I'm out to cut the junkie

With the plastic eyeballs, spray paint the vegetables

Dog food stalls with the beefcake pantyhose

Kill the headlights and put it in neutral

Stock car flamin' with a loser in the cruise control

Baby's in Reno with the Vitamin D

Got a couple of couches, sleep on the love seat

Someone came in sayin' I'm insane to complain

About a shotgun wedding and a stain on my shirt

Don't believe everything that you breathe

You get a parking violation and a maggot on your sleeve

So shave your face with some mace in the dark

Savin' all your food stamps and burnin' down the trailer park

Yo, cut it

Soy un perdedor

I'm a loser, baby, so why don't you kill me?

(Double barrel buckshot)

Soy un perdedor

I'm a loser baby, so why don't you kill me?

Forces of evil on a bozo nightmare

Ban all the music with a phony gas chamber

'Cause one's got a weasel and the other's got a flag

One's on the pole, shove the other in a bag

With the rerun shows and the cocaine nose-job

The daytime crap of the folksinger slob

He hung himself with a guitar string

A slab of turkey neck and it's hangin' from a pigeon wing

You can't write if you can't relate

Trade the cash for the beef, for the body, for the hate

And my time is a piece of wax fallin' on a termite

That's chokin' on the splinters

Soy un perdedor

I'm a loser baby, so why don't you kill me?

(Get crazy with the cheese whiz)

Soy un perdedor

I'm a loser baby, so why don't you kill me?

(Drive-by body pierce)

Yo, bring it on down

I'm a driver, I'm a winner

Things are gonna change, I can feel it

Soy un perdedor

I'm a loser baby, so why don't you kill me?

(I can't believe you)

Soy un perdedor

I'm a loser baby, so why don't you kill me?

Soy un perdedor

I'm a loser baby, so why don't you kill me?

(Sprechen sie Deutsche, baby)

Soy un perdedor

I'm a loser, baby, so why don't you kill me?

(Know what I'm sayin'?)

Both Alice and Baxter nod agreeing with David, who ate the last remains of his sandwich and said, “Well I’d better be leavin’ thanks for tuna sandwich. I’ll see you two around.”

With that David goes over to a window and climbs out.

Baxter let out a sigh, “I don’t know why he leave by using the front door like everyone else.”

Alice pats Baxter on the back, “Well then he wouldn’t be David would he.”

CHAPTER 5

Baxter and Alice's battered old heap of a car speeds along the road. One of the car's headlights keeps on going out on the driver's side, and there's only one windscreen wiper on the passenger's side. The car turns into a crescent of imposing Victorian houses. Pulls up and the pair get out.

Alice checks her dress before crossing the road. Baxter follows straightening his trousers. Parked opposite is a flash -looking sports car that looks immaculate. Alice looks approvingly as they pass. "This is Lady deMolay's car."

A brass head knocker in the shape of a naked lady goes into operation. Here's a sight. A wall with surreal kinky pictures with Lady deMolay stranding in front of it them. She holds a cute little dog in her right hand and a glass with wine in her left. She's delighted to see them. With a sweep of the dangling dog she ushers them in and the coats come off. Lady deMolay is a classy, and for her age quite sexy looking woman. She gives Baxter a long lingering look as he hangs up his coat. She goes up behind him. Almost on top him.

Lady deMolay in a sexy voice, "Would you like any help with that. I mean hanging your coat up?"

Lady deMolay has a very posh cultured (sexy) voice. Baxter almost drops his coat. He picks it up quickly and put it on the hanger and moves out of Lady deMolay's way.

Lady deMolaywaves her hand up and beckoned the two in, "Please, please make yourselves at home. Why don't you two go into the living room and sit down."

Alice and Baxter do as they're told. They enter a large living room, music plays in the background. Lady deMolay follows eyeing up Baxter's backside as does, "Would you two like a drink?"

Baxter puts in for a beer and Alice for a whisky with ice. Alice is obviously to be taken seriously. There's a trolley full of malt whisky here so she is out to make a good impression. Painting and tapestries decorate the walls.

Baxter is somewhat uncomfortable here, and Lady deMolay looking at him like she wants to rip his clothes off doesn't make him feel any more comfortable. Alice in complete contrast is totally at ease with these surroundings. Apart from the magnificent furniture the room is filled with CD's and videos and books. Baxter looks over at some of the rows of books. Lady deMolay notices him looking.

Lady deMolay asks cheerfully, “Do you like to read Baxter?”

Baxter nods shyly, “Yes. Very much.”

Aunty lets out a high laugh and then stopped as suddenly and stared Baxter full in the face, “I have books on every part of love making from around the world.”

Lady deMolay gives Baxter a big sexy smile. Baxter looks at Alice for help. Alice smiles back sweetly at him, trying not to laugh at his expression.

Alice turns to Lady deMolay, “Do you still erm… collect film’s Aunty?”

Lady deMolay nods very quickly this was clearly a subject close to her heart, “Oh yes. I’ve got tons of porn now. There was this one I was watching last night. Had this man in it. Arse so tight he was bouncing all over the place.”

Alice lets out an uneasy laugh, “I meant are you still collecting those old black and white classics?”

Lady deMolaylet out a little laugh. She gives Alice and Baxter their drinks. She gives Baxter a wink as he hands him his. She turns to Alice and shook her firmly, “Heavens no. I don’t collect rubbish like that anymore. No nowadays

I like porn. The really hard stuff! The harder the better. You only live once don't you my dear. Must to make the most of life while you can."

Baxter exchanges looks with Alice. As if to say "please get me out of here'. Lady deMolay doesn't notice this exchange of looks, she's too busy lifting up her skirt. She addresses Alice and Baxter with mock shock, "Oh dear look what's happened. I seem to have got a rip in my stockings."

Alice and Baxter look up to see there is indeed a rip in Lady deMolay's stockings.

Aunty went to the front room's door, "Can you two excuse me for a moment? I'll just go and change these. Won't be long. Help yourself to drinks."

With out much a do Lady deMolay takes off her skirt in front of Alice and Baxter and evaporates from the living room with a giggle towards Baxter.

Alice smiles at Baxter, "So far so good ah?"

Baxter looks at as if she totally is insane, "I want to go home right now! That aunty of yours if mad!"

Alice leaps to her feet and goes over to the drinks trolley. She downs several huge gulps of whisky from a bottle and then offers Baxter some. Baxter goes over takes a long gulp, "I mean it Alice I want to go home. That woman's mad."

Alice shook her head with a bright smile, "Eccentric."

Baxter not wanting to hear anymore, "Eccentric! She's insane! Not only that, she's a raving sex manic."

Alice snapped back at her friend, "Oh don't be daft. She's just an offbeat sense of humour. Just relax will you."

They reseat at speed and attempt to look relaxed. A moment later Lady deMolay's little dog comes skidding out, followed by Lady deMolay, who is now in nothing but very sexy black underwear. She doesn't seem to notice Alice and Baxter's bewildered expressions, as she rushes after the dog with a scream, "You little shit of a fur ball, I'm going to cut off your nuts and paws. Bastard!"

A degree of surprise from Baxter and Alice as Lady deMolaygoes after the dog. It shelters behind a chair and she concedes to its agility. Wiping sweat from her brow she sits next to Baxter. She reaches out and places her hand on his knee, as Alice asks, “Ah shall I get you another drink Aunty?”

Lady deMolay looks over at the dog as it pops its head around the chair.

Lady deMolay hisses, “I hate that fucking dog, pisses everywhere, and the shit he does, the shit!”

She looks up at Alice with a smile, while her hand pats Baxter’s knee, “Yes, yes, yes please dear girl. You can get me a strong little whisky. But not too little, don’t hold back fill the glass, and no ice! And you must tell me the news. I haven’t seen you in years. Last I heard you were getting into acting.”

Alice smiles, “Yes that’s right. Well I’m still waiting for my big break. I sent off a screenplay a few weeks ago. Might hear something about that soon. And Baxter’s is soon doing an audition for rep.

Lady deMolay looks at Baxter wide -eyed, “Really. So you’re a thespian too?”

Alice with such a forces smile it was surprising it doesn’t break, “Lady deMolay used to act.”

Lady deMolay pretends to look shocked but it was clear she wanted to say her bit, “Oh, I’d hardly say that. It’s true I did act. In lots of porn really. Hard work all of it, I used to be so stiff from a day’s work I couldn’t walk for weeks. Oh men, those big well-endowed men. Yummy.”

Lady deMolay’s hand creeps up Baxter’s leg, “Alas now “I just have memories and quite a few toys.”

And one of those memories is on a crowed mantelpiece. A photograph of Lady deMolay in her youth holding a carrot. Lady deMolay stands and almost clasps the photo frame, she carried on speaking now rubbing Baxter’s knee harder, “Back in my youth I could get any man, or lady. I never was fussed with the finer points, but no longer. Time goes by so quickly you don’t know it’s gone before it’s too late.”

She turns and looks back at Baxter, her sexy voice hard with emotion, “Don’t you agree?”

Alice gently cuts in, “I hope I get to perform the parts I want? And I hope Baxter gets to perform the parts he wants.”

Lady deMolay claps her hand, “Oh you both will! And you’ll both be marvellous,”

Lady deMolay suddenly starts to rant out her story, seeming to forget that Baxter and Alice were even there, Baxter has had enough of this. He gets up from his seat and moves over to Alice and whispers, “Let’s get out of here, come on. She’s completely mad. Any minute now she going to start taking her clothes off and howling at the moon.”

Alice thinking fast, “Okay. Okay. Gimme a minute.”

Baxter firmly, “Either we get the money and the house in the country or we’re out of here.”

Alice is persuaded and approaches Lady deMolay who turns sad -eyed.

Alice gently, “Could I have a word with you Lady deMolay?”

Lady deMolay looks up startled as if remembering her had guests, “Forgive me, forgive me. I was recalling days when the grass was greener the wine sweeter, the sun longer in the sky etc, and these little things” Points to a novel next to her on the coffee table. “Let me read to you”, she says batting her eyelashes at Baxter…

In a seductive voice she reads…

The elegant young lady with beautiful piercing eyes glanced at her reflection with a sigh. Was it really her fault that every man in Paris wanted her divine, slender, elegant soul for themselves? Why just the other night she had bedded the King's position, maid and a few servant girls but still her lust wasn't satisfied. Was anybody within the land that could satisfy her longing? That's when she had heard about the mysterious stranger called Giacomo Casanova. This gentleman it was said could charm a nun out of her underwear. Well, she thought, she would like to see him try his charms on herself. She paused by gently stroking her perfectly round breasts and tilted her head as she glanced into the mirror. Then there was the other deviant that she had heard of. One Marquis de Sade. It was said that he was the most vile of seducers, praying on young innocent virgins and making them do unspeakable acts of deprived sincerity upon himself. She smiled a sly smile, well then, she thought, perhaps it was long overdue to meet these two individuals and see if they could handle the charm of Madame de Pompadour.

Casanova was yet again in trouble. The Nun before was telling him how much she loved him and wanted his babies, quite a few babies in fact. So Casanova did what most men would do and said bye and jumped out of the window to another shag. Who next? Well there was that pretty young 17-year-old with the tight butt and cute face. He'd had enough of Nun's for a while. He thought about the whole thing, and it surprised him to find he was bored. He must be getting old he thought but on seeing two very pretty ladies walk past him, and the size of the thing in his pants grow, he put a stop to the 'I'm getting old' act. What he really needed was a lady with the same passion for life he had. But where to find such a lady. He took out a bottle of wine that he had stolen from the Nun's place and drunk, thinking things over. Nope he couldn't think of a single lady that could keep up with him.

Maybe a quickie before dinner might help him find a way out from this boredom. He ran a hand through his hair and made sure there was nothing on his teeth and hurried up and caught up with the two ladies.

Elsewhere Marquis de Sade, looked at the blind folded girl in front of him that was seeing to him between his legs, and found he was bored. Bored of all things! The girl before was heaven sent, just a little over 17 and begging for it. It had all become the same, pretty young thing, make her do this and that, and then write about it. Same thing in and out every day. He needed a lady that would fight him, and he in turn would make her beg him. Quite a bit of begging going on for sure but it would be fun. He bent the young girls head more forward into his lap…

Alice agrees and manoeuvres her to the sofa. Baxter wanders and stands by a kinky picture as Alice hits the old dear with a stiff drink. To much music and too far away to hear what is said. Baxter examines a table infected with silver -framed photographs. One of a little girl sitting on the lap of a very young pretty looking Lady deMolay. The little girl is clearly Alice.

Alice is suddenly on her feet and heading for the drinks. She shoots Baxter a glance, followed by a cheeky wink. Evidently she thinks she's pulled it off. The house in the country and the money are in the bag. Baxter is delighted and drifts back into the conversation.

Lady deMolay carries on with her rant, "Indeed I remember my first agent. Neil Harding. He was a dreadful little shit. He had an office four floors up and did he ever take a jump out of the window. No!"

Alice is pouring whisky. Confident she has landed her fish. Lady deMolayredirects her eyes to a hovering Baxter, “I’m told you are a writer too.”

Baxter can’t find any reaction here but a shrug and a shy smile. The smile disappears when Lady deMolayasks, “Do you write poems about sex?”

Baxter a little shocked, “No, I eh, wish I could. I write down my thoughts really.”

Lady deMolay nods as if understanding, “Are you published?”

Baxter lets out a shy laugh, “Oh no. Maybe one day I will be.”

Lady deMolay is about to say something when the dog reappears. For reasons best known to itself it throws itself at Alice barking. Lady deMolayrears to her feet, “The fucker! I hate that little mutt, always shitting and pissing and shitting,”

Swinging her arms wildly she makes towards Alice and the cat in a menacing stoop. Both manage to get out of the way. Swearing the aunty follows the animal to a corner where it snarls in horror. Lady deMolaytries in vain to cut off the dogs’ escape. Alice and Baxter watch in amazement as pursuit continues. Lady deMolay smashes through the living room and dog suddenly vanishes through the door.

Alice takes her arm and manages to escort her to the sofa, “Let me get you a top up,”

Lady deMolaylooks around as if still looking for the dog and says, “I’m really sorry but you’d better go. The night is ruined because of that insane mutt, I should have it’s nuts cut when it was a puppy.”

Everything is slipping away. Baxter doesn’t seem to care anymore. Despite all the work put in with this raving aberration he is prepared to leave instantly. So it seems is Alice. Then a change of thought. A change of gear. Alice asks gently, “Listen, Aunty, could I have a quick word with you in private?”

Lady deMolaylooks at her, preparing to say no. But Alice is earnest. Then with a smile she says “Yes of course dear Alice’ and allows Alice to shunt her toward an enjoining room.”

Baxter has no idea what the plan is. But even so isn’t entirely happy with it. He stares after them till the door shuts.

On that instant the dog reappears and lifts its leg and pisses on the floor. Baxter eyes it with animosity. But the thing is no longer of importance. Finishing his whisky, he finds himself at a window. Night and moonlight and lights of other houses, in a way the view relaxes Baxter.

Baxter thinks to himself, “How many more maniacs out there? Nurturing porn films and poems about sex. Living in luxury houses with paranoid dogs terrified by sex crazed Aunties? Possibly thousands. Those with money are eccentric. Those without. Insane.”

The door suddenly opens. Lady deMolayout first. Considerably mellowed out and showing stabilisation. Alice next wiping her mouth. Doesn’t meet Baxter’s eyes but walks straight into the hall for her coat. Baxter swaps a smile with Lady deMolayand follows Alice out of the house grabbing their coats as they go.

Glad to be out of Lady deMolay’s house, the two friends take in the cold night air. Alice gives Baxter an enigmatic smile. Baxter smiles back trying to look just as enigmatic but gives up after a second.

After a moment, Baxter asks, “Well what did she say?”

Alice holds up her hand, a smug smile on her face, a large iron key dangling from her finger.

Alice smiles brightly, “We have the house and the money to boot.”

Baxter lets out a laugh of joy and hugs Alice as she joins in laughing with him.

CHAPTER 6

A greasy little back -street dungeon. Baxter and Alice’s car is shoulder height on a hydraulic jack. Alice and Baxter watch while a little Mechanic no more than a dwarf pokes beneath it with a 100 -watt bulb in a little wire cage. Doesn’t like what he sees. Stubbing his butt, he emerges to address Baxter, “Well it won’t be cheap to fix this mess up. You’re looking at around Â£200.”

When hearing the price Baxter exclaims in shock, “Â£200 pounds! We could buy a new car for that.”

The mechanic clearly bored just put the two friends straight, “Listen you two, this car here is unroadworthy. I’ve seen better tyres hanging over the side of a rug.”

Alice isn't happy with the way the mechanic was talking to them, "Nonsense it's lasted us for years. It's in first - class condition. Right get it down; we'll service it ourselves."

The Mechanic looks at them in horror, "Listen sweetheart this car here is a death-trap. It'll either end up killing you or someone else."

Alice smiles sweetly at the Mechanic, "First off I'm not your sweetheart. Second I don't like the way you've been looking at my tits all afternoon. Now like I said we'll service the car ourselves."

The Mechanic looks at Alice in shock for a moment then smiles, "Okay then I'll lower the car so you can go, Madam."

Sometime later the two friends were listening to music and a bit of drizzle was about. Baxter and Alice's rumbles in and they dismount. Alice opens the boot, shouting mechanical instructions at Baxter, "Right, you service the water and I'll service the tyres. Then you service the battery and then we'll get to the off -licence,"

A horrible dirty old man in a horrible old suit two decades late, This is the slimly Owner of the local off -licence. Alice and Baxter carry box loads of beer, wine and whisky to the counter. The Owner gives Alice a creepy grin, "I hope you have money for all that? But if you haven't got enough you could always make an old man very happy if you follow my meaning."

He gives Alice a hideous wink. Baxter doesn't believe what he's hearing and is about to have a right go at the dirty old basted when Alice speaks, "As a matter of fact we do have the money."

She takes out a wad of cash from her pocket and carries on speaking, "And if you ever speak to me like that again, I will come behind that counter and cut off you're nuts and make you eat them. You pervert."

The Owner lets out a cry and faint dead away. Baxter and Alice look over the counter and see the Owner staring at them blankly and covering his manhood.

Baxter looks shocked, "You don't think he's dead do you Alice?"

Alice takes another look at the shop Owner. After a bit she shakes her head, "No. He's coming too."

Alice leaves a pile of money on the counter.

"Right let's go before he gets a hard on."

With that Alice and Baxter carry out they're boxes of booze.

From somewhere behind the counter the owner cried out, "Help. Someone help. I think I've just shat in my pants."

The song from somewhere could be heard a loud high-energy version of the classic song "The passenger' begins, A fucking great demolition ball in action, puts one into the belly of a wall and it collapses like a drunk. Much rubble and dust. As it draws back for another blow the camera moves with it and keeps moving on to Baxter and Alice's car. Baxter already inside with a bottle of whisky. Alice gets into the driving seat. He wears sunglasses. She starts the car and glances across the site. With a hand Alice runs her fingers through her fair hair, Baxter watches, There is something oddly sexy in the manner she does his. The car disappears into the traffic.

Music is playing loudly as Baxter and Alice drove through suburb wastelands of Southampton. A scraggy land of TV aerials and faces in corporate shock. Miles and miles of recently constructed high -rise slums. Each with its architecturally designed and resident -vandalised tree.

A roar from the punctured exhaust. They pass a line of schoolgirls at a bus stop. Baxter hanging from the windows, “You little tarts! You tart! Go forth and make babies and live off the social!”

Baxter clasps his bottle of booze. Laughing out and pissed as a gorilla.

Alice tries to control her patience, “Will you please try to calm down Baxter? Did you drop a pill before you came out or something?”

Baxter grins cheerfully and burps, “I took a few. Yes, I did! Those little tarts. They love it,”

Alice sighs and tries to talk sense into Baxter, “Listen to me Baxter. I’m trying to drive this thing as quietly as possible. You must calm down and try to relax. Otherwise we’re going to get stopped by the police. Gimme the bottle.”

Alice grabs the whisky. Takes a hit. Baxter grabs it back. Another guzzle at the bottle. And another exterior attraction. They pass a sign:

“ACCIDENT BLACK SPOT. DRIVE WITH EXTREME CARE. SOUTHAMPTON CITY ROADS.’

Baxter laughs insanely and points at the sign, “Look at that Alice! Look at that! Accident black spot! These aren’t accidents. They’re throwing themselves into the road!

Gladly! Throwing themselves into the road to escape all this hideousness."

Alice laughs and notices yob on a corner. The window goes down and Alice screams, "Throw yourself into the road, darling. The world hasn't got a chance."

The old car is giving ninety. Brutal rust on traffic -free road,

Factories and power stations and morbid industrial complexes...Alice and Baxter's car roars down the motorway as it does this we have an overhead view of the car and we hear them in voiceover, the land in ruins and so is the sky. Great greasy clouds are piling on the horizon. It'll be dark in less than an hour.

Baxter thinks to himself and asked, "Have we got anything to eat? I have a hole in my gut that needs filling."

Alice points to the dashboard, "There's some sandwiches in that brown paper bag on the dashboard."

Baxter looks at them fearfully, "What are they?"

Alice snaps, "What do you think? Tuna."

Baxter looks at one of the sandwiches horrified, "Shit! Alice these have sweet corn in them."

Alice not believing what she is hearing, “So what’s wrong with that?”

Baxter looks at Alice with bloodshot eyes and almost in a whisper said, “Sweet corn doesn’t agree with me. It makes me shit all night. And when I say shit, I mean the mother of all crap.”

Alice thinks of something to say to shut Baxter up, “Do you know they say sweet corn approves your sex drive? Just think when you get to the country, you might meet one of those sexy farm girls, like they have in those old movies.”

Baxter thinks for a moment and then grinned, “You know these sandwiches aren’t that bad.”

Alice laughs.

They pass bridges and other roadside bollocks.

The car hits the rain. Hardly any decrease in speed. Black and ominous -looking hills. Balls of black cloud rolling into a valley. The car descends with them. The brake lights come on.

As evening approaches Alice pulled over and climbs out. One hell of a gale is blowing. She gets to the passenger side of the car. Starts wrenching at the still -moving wiper blade.

Baxter's face is periodically visible. Wrecked in his seat and asleep with his jaw wide open. Alice fails to relocate the wiper blade. Soaking wet she staggers back to her door. Slams it with nothing achieved.

The force of Alice's entry wakes her co -pilot and navigator. Nothing but the beat of the windscreen wiper.

Half asleep he asks, "Are we there?"

Alice snapped angrily, "No dear we're not. We're here. Wherever here is. And we're in the middle of a shitting bloody gale."

She starts the engine and pulls out. She gives instructions to Baxter, "You'll have to keep a lookout your side. If you see anything, tell me. And hold that map."

Baxter emits an accelerating groan. Something to do with a headache. He looks across. Eyes like a pair of decayed clams and wondered, "Where's the whisky?"

Alice points downwards, "Down there by you're feet silly. You okay you look like shit, if you don't mind me saying so?"

Baxter groaned, “I’ve got a bastard behind my eyes. I can’t take aspirins with out a shot of whisky.”

He discovers a bottle of drink, pops the cork and passes it over to Alice after having a big gulp himself first, “Where’s the aspirins?”

Alice thinks for a moment, “Probably in the bathroom at home.”

Baxter looks at her, “You mean we’ve come out in the middle of bloody nowhere without aspirins?”

This appears to be the case. Baxter is becoming emotional.

Alice tries to change the subject, “I wonder where the hell we are?”

Baxter answers sarcastically, “How the hell should I know where we are? This was your idea remember. A holiday in the fucking countryside. God I feel like a pig has shat in my head.”

Alice is in no mood for one of Baxter’s over -the -top scenes of emotion. She turns and speaks firmly to Baxter, “Get hold of that map, and look for a place called Wicker Point.”

Baxter cries out theatrically, “I can’t. I’ve gone blind. My bladder’s exploding. I’ve got to have a slash.”

Alice a little annoyed, “Well you can’t Baxter. You’ll have to wait.”

Baxter horrified at the suggestion, “What do you mean I’ll have to wait? I’ve got to have a slash Alice. Stop this bastard of a car and let me out.”

Alice really starting to lose her temper, “Will you please stop being so silly and stupid? Look at the map. Find a biro cross.”

Baxter grabs it. Practically destroys it. Approaches a shout, “We’re about a yard from Southampton, and going up a hill! Now for Christ’s sake, stop this crate and let me out.”

The night is overpoweringly black. Towards the end of his monumentally long piss Baxter turns to Alice, “I think all this is a mistake. A serious and soon -to -be -regretted mistake. God know what happens in and around these parts. Have you ever seen the that horror film the Wicker Man, my God we’re going to place called Wicker Point? What does that tell you?”

Alice starts the car and let out a sigh, “I don’t know my dear Baxter. What does it tell us?”

Baxter replies grimly, “That the fucking omens aren’t good about this trip or holiday, or whatever you want to call it.”

As if to add to the point Baxter is making, lightning flashes across the dark heavens.

The car winds up a maze of stonewalls,

The vehicle passes a concealed entrance. Backs up to reveal a sign saying Wicker Point Farm. Takes this turning.

The car passes through Wicker Point Farm and continues.

The old car bumps down a rutted track in deep night.

Windscreen wiper battling the rain. A house comes into view.

Above the car as its headlights sweeps a bleak -looking cottage. At a glance picturesque. Mud conspires to prevent Alice’s sharp right -angled turn into the yard. The car slides into the gate. A crank of a handbrake and they get out.

Baxter says dramatically, “There must and shall be aspirin,”

Alice levers a pair of suitcases and grocery bags from the car. Violent rain sweeps through the headlights of the car. There is a load pop and the headlights go out. Baxter hangs over the partially open gate like laundry, “If I don’t get aspirin, I shall die, here, on this fucking mountainside.”

Staggers, groaning, to the front and gets pushed gently aside by Alice, “Come on now. Stop your moaning and give me the key. Let’s get you inside and I’ll get you a fix of sugar. You’re getting hyper again.”

The door opens, revealing a smudge of moonlight from outside, Alice strikes a match and Baxter whispers, “Christ Almighty.’ In the instant before the match goes out they see crumbling walls and stale shadows and giant atlases of damp on the floor. They also see an oil lamp. The match goes out. Another is lit. A yellow glow and the lamp reveals all. Table with several chairs.

Old but not antique... There are also two armchairs and a chaise -lounge with stuffing hanging out. A grate. Alice journeys into an adjoining room. Checks stairs and turns back to a sink with a rusty pump. She drags the lever down. A rheumatic whine. No water. The wind howls like wolves. She moves back into the kitchen and discovers Baxter sitting in a chair.

Alice asks, “What are you doing?”

Pair of shocked and red -shot eyes focus in her direction, "Sitting down to enjoy my holiday." Blasts of icy intensity rocket down thc chimney. Alice checks out a huge range and turns back to Baxter forcing the optimism, "All right, we're gonna have to approach this scientifically. First thing is to get a fire alight. Then we'll split into two facts - finding groups. I'll deal with the water and other plumbing's. You can check the fuel and wood situation."

CHAPTER 7

With an abundance of acrid smoke, a small fire smoulders in the grate. Baxter and Alice stare into the fire. From somewhere fucking cold wind in coming in throughout the cottage, at every change of the cold air they are engulfed in smoke.

This place is fucking uninhabitable.

Baxter lets out a sigh, as if to say "What the hell are we doing here' Alice notices the sigh and snaps, "Give it a shitting chance. It's gotta warm up."

Baxter grumpily replied, "Warm up? We may as well be sitting around a fucking cigarette."

Alice takes a large slug of whisky. Hands it across. Baxter practically finishes it. Lights a cigarette and starts coughing as he's temporarily obscured by another air blast of smoke, "This is ridiculous. We'll be found dead in here next spring. I've got a blinding fucking headache. I must have heat Alice."

Alice lets out a sigh and walks over to Baxter. She puts her arms around Baxter and holds him tight, "What are you doing?"

Alice gently says, “Don’t talk and just relax, I’m sharing my body heat with you. That should heat you up,”

Baxter though a little uncomfortable with this lets himself relax. And in a while drifts off to sleep while Alice hums a sweet tune. There is something almost magical about the moment, until Alice lets out a loud fart,but Baxter doesn’t notice and carries on sleeping and soon drifts off into a rather strange dream,,

, Baxter and Alice are in a strange creepy old bar. A teenager shot up to the eyeballs on drugs in kicking the crap out a jukebox and a hunting version of Massive Attacks “Safe from Harm’ plays in the background. Alice is eyeing up a barkeeper and winks at him. The barkeeper notices and gives her a Hollywood smile, Baxter doesn’t seem to like this one bit and spits at him. Alice gives Baxter a look and snaps, “Could you a fucking dear and stop spitting at Brad Pitt,”

For the Barkeeper really is the Hollywood hunk Brad Pitt.

Baxter starts to sulks and puts his middle finger up at Brad as he keeps on smiling at Alice.

Baxter sarcastically said, “He may have loads of money Alice and good looks but you can be sure of one thing,”

Alice cuts in dreamily, “And what would that be my dear Baxter?”

Baxter even more sarcastically, “He has a small dick and is most likely gay,”

Suddenly Baxter and Alice are at a table with an Alien and a Predator, Alice looks at them with a stare, “I don’t like the look of these two, I don’t think they like each other very much.”

Baxter looked worried, “Yeah they look like real hard nutsier think we’d better move to another table before things get out of hand.”

No sooner as Baxter said this that The Predator fire a laser blast at the Alien.

The Alien stands up to its good eight foot in height and lets out a hiss, slime running out of its mouth, some of which spills into Alice’s beer; Much to her dismay, “Well some people have no manners!”

The Alien flips its tail and knocks both Alice and Baxter from the table.

Baxter pops his head over the over turned table, “Well I guess that told us didn’t it Alice?”

Alice pops her head up as well, her fair hair covered with spilled beer, “Yes it did.”

One of the people in the crowd tries to calm the Alien and Predator down, and Predator picks up the person and breaks him into two and throws him aside without a second thought. The Alien picks up a beer and takes a swig and spits it out at the rest of the people in the bar, who start to scream in horror.

One man tries to throw a dart at the two of them. But as you can tell this doesn’t really have any affect over two eight foot aliens. The alien rips a hole through the man with the dart with its tail.

The Predator head butts the Alien and it falls back onto a jukebox and “Two Tribes, The “94 remix’ starts to play as the two breasts start to kick the crap out of each other.

Baxter and Alice watch eating peanuts while doing so, “My money’s on The Predator.”

Baxter intrigued, “Why?”

Alice excitedly, “Have you seen the size of that things cod piece, it’s huge!”

Baxter takes a look and sighs, “I see what you mean, that thing is huge.”

The Predator stops fighting the Alien and does a little dance to the music that is playing on the jukebox, the Alien shakes it’s head to the music as well, then they both stop and start fighting again.

Alice watches this with bemusement, “Must be a love hate thing.”

Baxter nodded, “Yeah, they love to hate each other.”

By now the whole bar is getting smashed to pieces and everyone is screaming.

One loud old fat woman sat on a stool by the bar screams out things in between drinking her pint, louder than the others, looking bored, “GOD SOMEONE STOP THEM, THEY”RE GOING TO KILL EACH OTHER!”

She stops drinking takes another mouthful of beer from her pint and then starts to screaming again, “PLEASE SOMEONE STOP THEM, THEY”RE LIKE MAD INSANE MANICS, WILL ANYONE HELP?”

Then she stops screaming looking bored again and carries on drinking her pint, when,

A powerful distinguished voice answers from nowhere, “Enough of this childish behaviour!”

Everyone in the bar turns towards the voice. Alice and Baxter notice a tall elderly figure stood framed in the front door of the bar. After what seems like a life, the figure steps forward and the effect is unbelievable everyone kneels before the old gentleman.

Baxter and Alice look at each other and shake their heads as if to say “Well that country folk for you’ and return to their pint.

Then Alice stops drinking suddenly and looks up, Baxter notices and follows her gaze, and sees, that the old gentleman is now stood by their table. His icy cold brown eyes, glaring down at them,

A beat

Then he speaks, his voice like silk, “I take it you and your lovely young lady friend here are new to Wicker Point, otherwise you would know what an act of blasphemy it is not to kneel before me, Lord Summarise, or if you prefer Lord Saruman”

The old gentleman almost shoots the last part. .

Right now Baxter is shitting himself and looks at Alice for help. Alice takes a sip of her pint and stares back at the old gentleman coolly. She answers back sweetly, "I was under the impression that you were an actor called Christopher Lee,"

Christopher Lee answered gravely, "I have many names my young lady,"

Alice looks thoughtful, "I thought Saruman was in Lord of the Rings, there isn't a Lord of the Rings film that I know of."

Christopher Lee answered proudly, "Not yet but there will be. And I shall be in it, now could you be a dear and let me terrify your friend Baxter here?"

Alice looked puzzled, "Why?"

Christopher Lee smiled creepily, "Because this is Baxter's strange nightmare not yours my dear Alice,"

Alice smiles, "Oh right. So it is. Go ahead scare the hell out of him."

Christopher Lee bowed and said, "Thank you my dear Lady."

Alice returns to her pint looks though and added, “I need the loo anyway. Number two calling if you get my drift.”

With that Alice leaves and heads towards the ladies. Christopher Lee turns back to Baxter looks thoughtful for a moment, “Now where was I , oh yes , I remember.”

He points a finger back at Baxter and hisses, “What brings you to Wicker point?”

Baxter looks ready to jump out of his skin and then wets himself like a fish in water when Christopher Lee roars, “, Tell me now boy!”

Baxter answers with a scream, “We came here to get drunk and stoned and so I could get laid with some fair- haired country farm girls.”

Christopher Lee stares hard at Baxter with his eerie brown eyes, he waves over to the barkeeper, who comes over and hands Christopher Lee a glass of red wine, he takes a sip and carries on staring at Baxter.

Alice returns and lets out a sigh, “God that feels better. Hate it when I have to carry a load inside me. To be honest I had to give a really good shove near the end. Bloody thing was a snake, just wouldn’t come out. But then I screamed like I was being made love too for the first time and out it went."

Alice looks at Baxter who is looking like he's about to have a heart attack while

Christopher Lee stares at Baxter sipping his wine.

Alice shakes her head. She picks up her pint, "Oh well just you and me then."

She raised the pint glass and starts to drink away.

Christopher Lee leans over the table and hisses with his face inches away from Baxter, "Do you know Mr. Baxter I know everything and more! And right now I sense the dark side of unrequited love inside you Mr. Baxter. It could be the drugs that you take to forget."

Baxter looks confused, "Well yes I do drink and take drugs to forget."

He looks even more confused, "But I forget what it is I want to forget."

Christopher Lee roared, "Spare me child. You know why! You will find many strange things happen here at Wicker point Mr. Baxter,

Admit your true feelings before it is too late,

Do not suffer the fate of your friend David. You will find there as one who will guild you in Wicker point heed her words before it is too late,"

Alice breaks in Christopher Lee's speech. Looking up at him with puppy dog eyes, "You know you're really quite cute and sexy for an older guy. In fact you're really quite hot. "

Christopher Lee looks sideways at Alice and nods, "Thank you dear I suppose I am."

He turns back to Baxter and whispers in his ear, "Remember my words Mr. Baxter. Now wake up and don't forget the standard scream."

Christopher Lee's face changes into a demon/ devil. Take That member, you take your pick.

Baxter screams.

Baxter wakes up screaming and notices that he is naked. Outside through the window he noticed that it was already daylight. He notices a pile of cloths by his bed. He hears Alice downstairs humming to a tune as she cooks breakfast.

He pulls on some boxer shorts and a t- shirt and leaves the room.

Lotta rain since Shanna left—weeks and weeks of it. It seems forever since I've seen a blue patch of sky. Drops of rain pelt the tall windows of the old Manhattan loft I call home, the occasional clap of thunder echoing through the big empty apartment like a bass drum roll. I tend to sleep a lot these days. Otherwise I drink, smoke grass, write new songs, and try to catch a glimpse of the remnant ghosts of Shanna that always seem to linger in the periphery of my vision.

No, Shanna's not dead. She left me for a keyboard player. Yeah, that's right–keyboards.

No, Shanna's very alive and making music with that dude, and I'm left here with a lot of memories that manifest themselves as drunk/high phantasms of ethereal Shanna—her wearing my shirt while she makes me breakfast, lounging on the couch reading trashy novels, doing her yoga in her tights.

This morning I wake up, the remnants of a Technicolor dream adrift in my head. In it Shanna and I are hiking Kauai beneath a Pacific blue, cloudless sky, her red hair aglow in the morning sun. I pull her close for a kiss in the dream, but she vanishes like a dust mote drifting out of a shaft of sunlight. I try to slip back into the comfort of dream-time twilight, but it doesn't take, so I get out of bed and pick up my battered old Martin and strum a "G." The chord echoes through the loft like it owns the place. I set about writing another song. Inspiration. Song fodder. Shanna's still good for that.

***

I have a standing solo guitar gig at *Dean-O's Taki Lounge* in Alphabet City that pays for the rent and a few niceties like booze, pot and the occasional cheeseburger or slice. I open most nights for whatever name band they have, then hang around drinking until the wee hours, when I do a late-night set for whatever drunks remain. Tonight I walk there in the rain, guitar case in hand.

I play my set to disinterest from an unusually large crowd that fills the cave-like bar. The featured band is some new outfit called *The Regal Rogues* that I've never seen before. But *Dean-O's* books good talent, and as it's a Friday night, the house is hopping.

After my set I take a seat at the bar and sip the first of many free drinks that the bartender sends my way. I watch *The Rogues'* roadies set up their gear. Roadies! Nice little luxury if you can afford it. I scowl when I see them set up a couple of Roland keyboards. Shit. Maybe I'll go get some dinner somewhere else.

But the booze here is free, so I stay. Soon enough the band comes out and starts to play. I'm almost not surprised when the keyboards are manned by Shanna's new boyfriend, Dirk. Shanna, of course, is on lead vocals.

She's dressed in tight black leather pants and a bustier, a startling combination with her brilliant red mane. She rocks, dances and gyrates as she sings. The crowd loves her and her pitch-perfect voice, mellifluous as the rain. Shanna loves the rain. I just then remember that. I wonder if the fact that there's been so much of it is her parting curse on me.

Halfway through her set she notices me at the bar. She shoots me a *Cheshire Cat* smile, her green eyes warm and bright. I crawl down inside my gin and try to ignore her.

After her band is finished she comes over. "Hey Gene." Her rich voice makes it seem the bar and all the world have gone silent.

"Shanna."

"Hey, I been meaning to call you. I played your demo for a guy at Capitol. He dug it. If I can find his card, I'll email you his number."

"Great."

Just then Dirk Keyboards comes over. He puts a thin, skeletal hand on her shoulder. "Hey baby, let's get outta here, I'm starved."

"In a minute. I'll meet you outside."

"Okay, don't be long."

He goes and we have awkward silence for a moment. "Drink?" I finally ask her.

"Nah, I quit."

"Really?"

"Yeah…I'm…well, I'm trying to be healthy."

I glance at her belly—a bit less taut than usual beneath her bustier. "Okay." I try to stifle a bit of anger as this tells me she must have begun her relations with Dirk Keyboards a bit earlier than I'd realized, before we'd finished ours. We'd always been careful about such things.

"Look, Gene. I'm sorry it worked out like it did. I really miss you sometimes."

"I miss you too."

"Well, we can be friends, right?"

"Sure, why not."

"Great. I'm gonna send you that number. You're gonna do great. I know it."

She hugs me and I smell her peach blossom perfume and feel the warmth of her bare shoulder and soft skin and birds fly and fireworks explode and the sun goes nova and a song forms in my heart that says *let's run away and never say that we don't love each other anymore.*

"I gotta go," she says, pulling free. "You take care."

"Sure, Shanna, sure."

She goes. The bar noise ramps up again like the cacophony of a scratched vinyl record.

I play my last set and then sit at the bar drinking gin until dawn. When I leave I stumble out of the place. Bright sunlight shines down the canyon of Fourteenth Street. I look up between the building tops and see for the first time in weeks an utterly clear patch of blue sky. The rain is gone, and so is Shanna. The blue sky tells me this as much as anything else.

CHAPTER 8

Alice is busy at the cooker cooking some black stuff in a frying pan.

David sits at the table rolling up a cigarette and eyeing Alice's backside.

Baxter makes a face at the sight of the stuff in the frying pan. He walks past David, "Morning Dave."

Baxter goes over to the fridge and takes out a pint of milk and starts to drink it out of the carton thinking for a moment then spits out his milk and turns around to face David, "How the fuck did you get here?"

David finishes rolling up his cigarette lights it and stares up at Baxter, "Nice boxer shorts man."

Baxter still confused, "Never mind my fucking boxers. How the fuck did you get here?"

David looks thoughtful for a moment and after good five minutes answers, "Well it all happened the night before last. I was wandering around and I had nowhere to sleep. I was going to climb through your window at your place in Southampton but the windows were all locked so I noticed the boot of your car was open. So I decided to sleep in there instead. Next thing I know I wake up and see Alice looking down at me, asking if I want some breakfast and saying what a lovely surprise it was to find me in the boot."

Baxter looks thoughtful for a moment, "Oh that's fine then. That all makes sense,"

Alice doesn't seem to have heard any of this and starts to laugh, "Hey David they're playing your song."

David who was still looking at Alice's arse wondered, "What would that be Alice?"

Alice replied cheerfully, 'National crime awareness week' by Sparks. I was thinking after breakfast we all could go for a walk into the country. See the rest of Wicker Point and taking the local sights."

Baxter is about to answer when he stops drinking of the carton of milk and makes a face, "What's wrong with this milk? It has lumps in it."

Alice grins, "Oh I forgot the milk is off. Just imagine its yoghurt."

Baxter shrugs, "Okay."

He carries on finishing the bad milk from the carton.

Alice thinks for a moment then comes up with a suggestion, “Maybe you could go and see the neighbour in the next cottage a little away from here. They may have some fresh milk.”

Baxter sulks, “Okay.”

Alice gives Baxter a quick hug, “Then after that we all could go for that walk I was talking about before.”

Baxter a bit more cheerful, “Okay.”

Alice and Baxter stare at David for an answer, David takes a dead rose from the flower vase on the table and starts to eat it. He notices the two of them staring at him and gives them his reply, “Okay.”

Baxter walks up to the doorway of a posh cottage. He pushes the doorbell and a David Bowie tune plays, the tune being “Space oddity’. The door opens and Baxter’s cigarette falls from his mouth.

For their standing in front of him larger than life is the legend himself, David Bowie.

David Bowie grins at Baxter and greets him. He has a strange way of speaking, in the way that he sorts of speaks and sings his sentences. From behind the open doorway we can hear the song “Hello Space boy’ by the Pet Shop Boys and David Bowie play loudly while this scene unfolds,

David looks at Baxter without expression, “Hello space boy!”

Baxter looks at him in amazement, “Oh my God, you are David Bowie!”

David Bowie smiles looking somewhat odd, “Yes, it is indeed me. I have lived here for quite a while. This isn’t America but it’s home.”

Baxter still not quite believing that he’s in fact talking to Bowie, “Ah Don’t you find it a bit creepy here Mr. Bowie?’

David Bowie looks thoughtful for moment then answers in a sing-along-voice, “No in fact I like scary monster’s super creeps.’

Baxter is about to ask something when David Bowie’s mobile phone goes off, “Excuse me for a moment.”

Speaks into his mobile phone, “Hello earth control calling Major Tom.”

David Bowie listens for a moment than answers, “Right I will call Mick; I think he is dancing in the USSR.”

He turns off the mobile phone and puts it away and grins at Baxter, “What is your name kid?”

Baxter answers, “Baxter”

David Bowie looks at him closely, “Do you like comics Baxter?”

Baxter thinks for a moment, “Don’t mind them.”

David Bowie closes his eyes and says again in a sing-along-voice, “I love them. I think we all should be heroes for a day. Tell me do you believe in aliens?”

Baxter starts looking a bit frighten now. He grins at David Bowie in an uneasy way, “Listen Mr. Bowie I don’t mean to be rude but I was just wondering if you have some fresh milk?”

David Bowie doesn’t seem to hear what Baxter is saying and stares off into the distance and starts to speak to himself, “I was thinking last night about loving the alien and asking her to put on her red shoes and saying let’s dance my little china girl. And all I could see was ashes to ashes and Ziggy Stardust was there. They all start to shout at me “Jump’ they say (starts to shout) “Jump’ they say.”

Baxter has enough. He notices some milk bottles on the doorstep. He picks them up and runs away like mad not daring to look back.

David Bowie comes out of his strange behaviour and looks around, “Where is that nice boy gone? Strange, all my neighbours seem to disappear after a while. Must be something about me. It’s confusing these days.”

With that he steps back in his house and closes the door.

CHAPTER 9

Alice, Baxter and David are walking through beautiful countryside the countryside scenery looks magnificent and wonderful. David is taking mouthful of pills, Baxter is smoking a joint where Alice takes photographs with a camera and shares the joint with Baxter at the same time, "So what was our neighbour like then?"

Baxter takes a drag of his joint and answers dreamily stoned as a hippie from the 60's, "He is a complete psycho. Oh and he is David Bowie by the way."

Alice and Baxter start laughing like mad, "David Bowie, of course he is, this must be good pot you're out of your head."

Baxter still giggling manages to say, "Yeah my head is spinning."

All three look at each other and burst onto a fit of giggles and laughter. Then David has an idea, "Hey, if we all lay down in the grass we all could look up in the sky and see if we can make out things in the shapes."

They all lie down in the grass and stare up at the clouds. Baxter is the first one to speak after a few moments, "I think I can see a man making love to a woman from behind up on that cloud on the right."

The cloud Baxter is looking at does indeed look like this.

Alice starts to giggle, "I think I see a big smiley face staring down at me on that cloud in the centre."

Alice's cloud indeed looks like this.

Baxter lets out a giggle, "Okay now I am bored, let's go and find a pub or some farm girls."

Alice grins, "Right you can have the farm girls I will have the farmer with his big tractor."

They get up to leave and start to walk away. Baxter stops and looks back and notices David is still lying in the grass and staring up in the sky.

Baxter asks, "You coming or are you staying here?"

David completely stoned replied, "You two go on ahead I meet you later."

They leave David lying on the grass staring at the sky trying to make out animals in the clouds. As they walk off they hear David shout, “I think I can see two rabbits trying to make babies up there.”

Alice and Baxter don’t take notice and walk off through the countryside. They come over a hill and they notice down the hill what appears to be a film crew and men in suits around some sort of large triangle- like objects.

Then they both, Alice and Baxter, notice a tall handsome man with boyish good looks dressed in a smart suit talking into a mobile phone.

Baxter and Alice look at each other in amazement, “My God is that who I think it is? Come on let’s find out.”

They both run off down the hill towards the man. Alice stares at him looking at him closely and then she lets out a childish laugh, “It is you, isn’t it? You’re David Duchovny. Or should I call you Fox Mulder?”

Alice and Baxter hear from somewhere a creepy version of the song “The hunter gets captured by the game’.

The man in the dark suit (who might be David Duchovny, but highly unlikely) looks around in an uneasy manner, “Ah yes, you can call me Mulder.”

Alice laughs like a child on Christmas day, "You tease you. So what are you lot doing here? Filming an episode of the X- Files here?"

The man looks confused, "What?"

Alice laughs, "You filming an episode here,"

She laughs again, "Or are you going to tell me, that really is a real clashed spacecraft there?"

She points at the object behind the man, where the other men in suits are working.

The man in suit/ Mulder gives Alice a blank look, "Yes, We're on filming a X- Files episode here, Ah what did you say you and your friends name were?"

Alice replies cheerfully, "Alice and Baxter."

The man is about to say something when he notices Baxter is nosing around the "UFO' prop, "Hey get away from there. That's not a toy."

Baxter waves back at him and moves away. A lovely female redhead appears and leads Baxter away.

In shocked excitement Alice shouts, "Oh my God that must be Scully!"

The redhead walks up to the man in the suit/ Mulder and whispers something in his ear.

Baxter and Alice look on and whisper among themselves, “Must be talking about how they’re going to act out there next scene.”

Baxter looked around as if to see if anyone was listening before he answered, “Yeah, hey guess what Scully gave me these pills. Said we were to take them tonight, as there’s some sort of flu or bug going around”

Alice giggles, “Yeah or they want us to forget that we ever saw anything.”

They both laugh again.

The man in the suit/ Mulder turns to them, “Well it’s been nice talking to you two, but we have a lot of, eh filming to do, so if you don’t mind,”

Baxter cuts in gently, “Oh that’s okay we’ll get out of your way.”

The sexy redhead tells Alice and Baxter, “Don’t forget to take those eh flu pills, just in case. I’m sure you don’t want to come down with anything.”

Alice grins like a teenager, “We won’t. In fact, we’ll take them now. If you can’t trust your heroes who can you trust eh?”

Alice and Baxter wave good-bye and walk away taking the pills.

After they have disappeared over a hill a creepy old cigarette smoking man walks over to the man in the suit/ Mulder and the Redhead/ Scully, “Do they suspect?”

The man in suit seriously answers, “No they think we’re filming a X- Files episode, it seems our cover story and our enhanced images seem to work.”

The creepy old cigarette smoking man takes a long drag on his cigarette and turns to speak to the redhead/ Scully, “Did you give them the memory blockers?”

She nods.

The creepy old cigarette smoking man nods back, “Good, all is going to plan, soon,”

The man’s speech is cut off short by his mobile phone going off, its loud ring tone being “Close Encounters of the third kind’

The creepy old cigarette smoking man lets out a sigh, "I really must change that ring tone."

Alice stops walking and looks at Baxter, "You know I have this strangest feeling that I have forgotten something really important."

Baxter looks at her in a glazed manner, "Yeah me too... All I know is that I have this overbearing urge to watch the X-Files tonight."

Alice nods slowly, "Yeah me too, hey wouldn't it be great if we could meet them? Mulder and Scully I mean."

Baxter just sighs sadly, "Fat chance. Nothing that exciting ever happens to us. Anyway do you remember what we were doing out here? Because I can't,"

Alice laughs, "No, Spooky maybe it's a case for Mulder and Scully."

Baxter nods solemnly and then grins, "Scully could do a case study or an autopsy on me anytime."

Alice laughs again, "And Mulder could probe me with an alien probe anytime he likes."

With that they both walk off giggling and humming the X-Files tune. As the day becomes night and stars shine down upon them.

CHAPTER 10

David is lying sleeping soundly on the grass.

From somewhere we hear the upbeat and uplifting song "Life is a flower' by Ace of base play,

A bottle of pills beside him labelled "Mega- LSD'

He opens his eyes suddenly and he looks around to see an amazing sight. There before him is a small Goblin and a Dwarf and beautiful winged fairies in sexy underwear.

David grins at his hallucination, "Hey, how are you lot doing? I haven't seen you guys in a long time. Come to think of it last time I saw you guys were back in the end of the 70's listening to Pink Floyd."

In his hallucination he imagines the creatures talking with subtitles from a foreign film.

The Goblin says, "God he is ugly, isn't he?"

The Dwarf nods agreeing, "Quick let's nick some stuff off him."

The Goblin grins, "I already have. I found a packet of condoms in his pocket. I think one of them was used; it was all wet and sticky,"

The Goblin turns and speaks to all of the fairies, "Hey ladies fancy some fun tonight?

I have got protection for a change,"

The Fairies answer altogether, "We would, but we have to leave some money for children who have lost their teeth tonight. We're all a bit broke so we'll do some overtime."

The Dwarf looks confused, "I thought that was the Tooth-Fairy's job?"

Again the Fairies answer together, "He is on strike, says he's not getting paid enough. He is fed up with getting dream dust for payment and he hates kids anyway. He calls them little shits."

The Goblin sighs, "Poor bastard I'd hate to have his job.

Right I'd better go down to do some work,"

The Goblin jumps onto David's chest and starts to jump up and down while the Dwarf picks up David's joint, which looks massive in the Dwarf's quite small hands and takes a puff. Smoke blows out of the Dwarf's ears and he goes up into the air like a rocket.

The Goblin stops jumping up and down as he notices that David has a big erection in his trousers, because he's getting a hard on watching the sexy fairies flying around him.

The Goblin's face becomes a mask of rage, "Why that pervert is eying up my girlfriends, right I'll teach him,"

The Goblin bites down hard on David's erection and David lets out a terrifying scream that men only dream of in their nightmares.

The Fairies start to pull the Goblin away, "Stop it he is not worth it! Remember your temper and your blood pressure!"

They drag the Goblin away while David holds his balls in agony. The Goblin screams at David while he is pulled away, "Bloody pervert! Next time I'll bring the Wicked Witch of the East to shove her broomstick up your arse!"

With that the creatures disappear.

A moment later the Dwarf falls down to earth and explodes into nothing.

David looks up at the night sky and says with Ecstasy, "God that was wonderful. I love female Goblins,"

He thinks for a moment looking worried, "Well I hope it was a female Goblin,"

David carries on giggling and laughing to himself as he looks up into the night sky.

CHAPTER 11

Baxter and David are watching a hard- core porn movie and Alice is knitting a jumper for some reason. She lets out a yawn and gets up, "Well I am going to go to bed. I'll see you tomorrow. Night boys."

Baxter and David sort of say good night but they are more interested in the porn films.

Alice shakes her head and thinks loudly, "Men! Always thinking with their penises."

She goes up the stairs to her room.

Alice lays in her bed, listening to the wind outside and slowly drifts off into a deep sleep which in turn changes a nightmare with creepy classical music that plays throughout the following dream sequence.

We're in a very large, gleaming department store, an eerie classical piece of music called "Violin Concerto 2nd movement' by Phillip Glass plays loudly on the department store's stereo speakers, which is eerily and completely black and empty. Dustbins with rubbish overflowing stand about as if they were a sign of doom, Alice notices an escalator some way from her,

She crosses over to it and takes in that it's moving. She stares up and sees nothing but blackness.

This is starting to scare and piss her off now, she lets out her anger in a scream, "This isn't fucking funny you know. If I find out I'm going to kick the shit out of you."

Then she starts to float up and she's humming a happy tune (we could have a creepy hammer film kind of music played out to this part of the sense mixed with an upbeat high- tech bass line, to give this whole nightmare sequence an even odder effect)

Now Alice is outside a strange clothes shop where incredibly creepy mannequins dressed in the worst awful clothes from every era stare at her. Alice walks by quickly and mutters, "The last time I saw anything as creepy as that lot was in old Doctor Who Episode, Or at one of David's parties,"

, Now we're in a small tidy café. Alice is sat down at one of the tables, which are made of glass, At the centre of Alice's table rests an ashtray, With a half- smoked joint burning away in it.

Alice looks around with a cheeky grin and picks up the joint in an almost childish manner, That's when an inhuman bonnily hand reaches out and takes the joint from her mouth.

Alice leaps out of her sect and looks up at the figure stood before her. A figure dressed in the blackest of robes, A hood covers his/ her/ it's face, hiding the face of the figure in shadow.

Alice watches, it seems to take a puff of the joint, It coughs suddenly in a loud inhuman way, Them slowly the thing raises its arm and it points at Alice, "Don't point at me it's rude to point, Whatever you are, Though I'm thinking psycho or some fucking nuttier."

Suddenly the hand of the figure is holding some sort of card. It moves over to her table and gently lays it down an Alice's table, Alice glances down and takes in that it's a tarot card with a picture of Death on it,

, Alice looks up and just for a brief moment she catches a glimmer of a horrific skull- like face beneath the hood,

The thing seems to sense and lowers the hood down back over its face.

Alice asks gently but yet intently, "Am I going to die?"

The hooded figure shakes its head.

Alice thinks hard and asks even more intently, "Who then? Baxter? My brother? Who?"

The figure moves into the shadows and seems to melt away. Alice screams after it as if it is the end of the world, "WHO?"

Alice wakes up with a start and manages to hold back a scream as she awakens from her nightmare.

She turns on the bedside lamp and lies there staring at the ceiling, shaking and sweating.

Then she hears a noise; somebody is coming upstairs outside her bedroom. The noise gets louder; footsteps can be heard outside her door.

Alice lies there, listening terrified for a few moments. Then she hears a scream from Baxter's room. Alice leaps out from her bed and looks around for a weapon. She picks up her lighter and flicks it on and then shakes her head if to say "What am I doing?' She looks around for a better weapon and jumps as Baxter screams again.

She picks up a chair but finds it a bit too heavy to carry and then she notices the baseball bat. She grapes it, goes to the bedroom door, counts to five, "1, 2, 3, 4, 5,"

She slams open the door and runs down the hallway to Baxter's room screaming like a psycho. She kicks open Baxter's door and stops in horror.

For they're on top of Baxter is Lady DeMolay. With nothing on apart from a yellow open raincoat that reveals extraordinary sexy underwear and stockings. Alice notices that Baxter isn't able to scream anymore because Lady DeMolay is trying to French- kiss him.

Although from where Alice is looking Lady DeMolay is doing all the work. Alice lets out a loud cough and Lady DeMolay freezes, her back away from Alice. She gets off Baxter and turns to face her niece. She looks ashamed and upset even to the point where she starts to cry, "Please dear child forgives me. I was driving by the old place and I decided to pay you a visit. I did knock but there was no answer so I broke a kitchen window and climbed in. What must you think of me?"

Alice looks kindly at her confused Auntie, "Please don't cry Auntie. You are just feeling ill. Did you take your happy pills tonight?"

Lady DeMolay looks confused and smiles, "Oh I knew I have forgotten something. You are such a sweet niece. You always were my favourite you know. I know people laugh at me, and who could blame them? I am a failed actress that loves carrots. But you have to understand I carry this sadness inside me, a sadness of someone who has never been loved or found true love. Can you imagine what it is like my dear child?"

Alice answers in a kind of voice, "I can only imagine Auntie. Please don't get upset you make yourself even worse. Why don't you get to sleep in the guest room tonight?"

Lady DeMolay shakes her head sadly and buttons up her raincoat with embarrassment, "No my dear Alice. I have made a fool of myself, and your friend Baxter here. I feel it is only right to tell you what I have decided a week ago.

I am going to leave you my cottage here in Wicker Point in my will but only on condition that if you meet someone that you truly love you tell him straight away how you feel.

Life is full of hit and misses of unrequited love my dear child; don't miss your chance Alice when you have your chance.

Be true to your heart and you will find the hits are greater than the misses most of the time."

Alice drops the baseball bat, eyes filled with gratitude at her Auntie's words. She rushes over and hugs her Auntie. Lady DeMolay hugs her back and then breaks away and leaves, goes downstairs and leaves the cottage.

CHAPTER 12

Lady DeMolay gets into her car and she sits behind the wheel and suddenly she bursts into tears.

She looks at a photo that is on the dashboard. She picks it up and looks at it.

The picture shows a handsome man smiling proudly.

Lady DeMolay turns on her car stereo and Erasure's "Spiralling' starts to play, this is the orchestral version and somehow fits in with the heart-breaking speech that Lady deMolay delivers, "I am sorry my sweet angel. I don't mean to do what I do, it's just that I never got over you leaving me after I lost the baby.

It wasn't my fault the Doctor said so. It was just one of those things which could happen any time to any woman in the early stages of pregnancy but you blamed me and you left saying I had denied you a son.

No wonder I keep on finding someone to replace you even though that I know that you stopped carrying when you didn't answer mw letter all those years and years ago but why would you I was only 15 at that time,"

With that she starts the car and drives off.

CHAPTER 13

Alice is standing by the window in Baxter's room and watches as Lady DeMolay's car speeds off.

Alice looks over to Baxter's bed and notices that her friend has passed out.

She gently shakes him and he awakes with a scream.

He looks up terrified at Alice, "I had this horrible dream that your Auntie Mo was trying to have it off with me."

Alice laughs and gets into bed with Baxter, "Just shut up and get back to sleep you were having a nightmare. I was having one too.

So I think it is only right we share the same bed just for tonight so we don't have any worse dreams."

Baxter thinks about it and nods his head, "Okay, fine by me. I hope you don't snore."

Baxter turns off their bedside lamp. There is darkness apart from the light from the moon shining through the bedroom window.

A moment later we see Alice leans over Baxter and turns on the light again. Baxter sits up and lets out a sigh,

“What’s wrong now Alice? I’m tired I wanna get some sleep,”

Alice sits up and stares into the distance as if troubled, “I need to talk some things over.”

There is a pause before Alice carries on concerned, “Have you ever wondered if taking all this drugs is good for us? I mean God knows what it is doing to our brains.”

Baxter looks puzzled at her, “What’s bought this on?”

Alice shakes her head and mumbles, “Nothing. It’s just that I think we are spending too much time drinking and taking drugs,”

She pauses again before carrying on, “I want to have a normal life someday you know, with a nice husband, maybe children,

I don’t want to be seen as another junkie left on the streets with nothing more than tears and bad memories.”

Baxter looks at the ceiling and agrees, “You know I feel the same way sometimes.

Sometimes I look at David and it rips me apart to see how he has become. You know that Christmas party a few years back, the one where Gabriel thought he was a Dalek.

I went upstairs to use the bathroom and found David sitting on the toilet crying his eyes out,

Did I ever tell you about that?"

Alice looks at Baxter surprised, "David was crying? I don't think I have ever seen him crying in his life."

Baxter suddenly looks very intently at Alice, "Yeah I was shocked as well as I saw him like that. I asked him what was the matter and first of all he said it was nothing and then I don't know why he told me everything,"

Baxter embarks on a flashback,

, From somewhere the incredibly moving song by Faithless called "I want my family back' plays,

David is sat on the toilet crying his eyes out his shirt off, revealing marks on his arms where he shut up. His whole arm's marked with them and there are large bruises on his body.

Baxter stands before him looking horrified at the sight before him.

David looks up at his friend with an ashamed expression on his face. He reaches down and takes a packet of cigarettes out of his jacket which lays down by his feet.

His hands are shaking so much that he drops the cigarette packet a few times and then manages to hold it long enough to take a cigarette out of it.

His shakes go even worse and he can't light his cigarette with his lighter.

Baxter gently takes hold of the lighter and helps his friend to light a cigarette.

He kneels in front of David and looks up kindly at his old friend, "What's going on David? It's not like you being like this, and where did you get all this bruises from?'

David takes a few nervous drags from his cigarette and starts to cry even more.

Baxter reaches out and holds David in his arms and David starts to speak slowly and painfully, "Sometimes I don't have enough money to pay my rent so the landlord throws me out until I have the money so I sleep in the park on benches.

The thing is when you get old troublemakers that come out of the clubs at closing time and they love nothing more than beating up homeless people.

Back in the old days I would have tried to fight back but now I leave them doing it.

They get bored after a while maybe they might just piss on you, take your money and leave you to die.

That's the nice ones; there are ones I could tell you about that would make you sick.

My father used to have it all a nice car a nice house my sister and me, we were the happiest children in the world and then my mother found him shooting up in the bathroom,

He was so ashamed that that Christmas he hung himself in the garden shed.

My mum told me that my dad had gone away for a while.

All I wanted was my family back,'

David stars to cry uncontrollable while Baxter holds him and David keeps on repeating himself over and over again, "I want my family back!'

After a while David just goes quiet and Baxter whispers in David's ear quietly and gently, "You do have a family. You have Alice and Gabriel and me until the day you die,'

Back in the present day Alice looks fondly at Baxter, "I never knew, that was sweet of you Baxter to say that to David. You surprise me sometimes you know,"

Baxter looks at Alice, "Surprise? How do you mean?"

Alice kisses him on his cheek and Baxter pushes her away embarrassed.

Alice looks upset and turns her head away and stares out of the bedroom window.

Baxter looks at her for a moment and realizes how beautiful she is for the first time and slowly and never so slowly he reaches out and holds her hand.

Alice turns to look at him,

They stare at each other for a moment. And for a moment we think they are going to kiss but just before the magic moment Baxter lets out a loud fart and they both break into giggles and laughter,

They both settle down to get to sleep and Baxter says half asleep, "Oh my God, I think she was trying to French- kiss me in my dream."

Alice giggles and soon they are both sound asleep.

CHAPTER 14

It is a bright sunny day in Wicker Point Village.

The place is lovely in an old fashioned sort of way. All the village people seem happy with their lives.

That is until Alice and Baxter's sorry excuse for a car drives into the village. The exhaust pipe letting out a horrible black smoke behind it. The car stops and the number-plate drops off.

Elsewhere in Southampton a sad story evolves…

I, Peyton Saunders, have a problem. I am used to having problems, like the wannabes at my school, but this is too big for me to handle. And the worst part is, I can't even talk to Addie and Jocelyn about this because they think I am totally ridiculous.
"Hey mom!" I said.
"Hey sweetie! How was school?" Mom asked.
"Good," I replied with a sigh. As I walked up my giant granite staircase, I pulled out my phone and I instantly text all of my friends. I plop on my huge, pink, queen sized bed and feel the warm fall breeze of Palm Springs, California. I

take a deep breath in, hold it for a few seconds, and then slowly puff out to relief the stress of another school day. As the phone rings, I don't even have to check the caller ID to know that it is a joint call with my best friends, Addie and Jocelyn. I pick up the phone to hear those two already gossiping. As I join in, we talk almost the entire night about things like boys, clothes, plans for the weekend, or whatever gossip the school day has brought us. We all go the Palm Springs High School. This is the typical after school routine for Addie, Jocelyn, and I.

The next morning, I wake up to the most annoying barking my dog has ever made. Taki is a Yorkshire terrier, and as cute as he is, his barking is getting out of control. As cruel as it sounds, I am seriously considering an electric collar. Once I finally got Taki to be quiet, I hop in the bathtub for a quick shower. I start to think about my outfit for today. Since it is Wednesday, I MUST wear pink so that helps me a little. Out of the shower and an hour and a half of hair and makeup later, it's time to get dressed. As I open the huge doors of my walk in closet, I know the perfect outfit to wear. I pick my Lucky Brand jeans, my pink Urban Outfitters t-shirt, my Tiffany necklace and charm bracelet, and my pink Louis Vuitton purse. I get dressed and am out the door to my pink Ferrari. I don't eat breakfast because it just makes me gain unnecessary carbs. I am out the door and on my way to pick up Addie and Jocelyn.

Once they get in the car we start to talk about cheerleading and the day ahead of us. Addie brings up the fact that we get our partners for our semester long science project today. I really hope I get either Addie or Jocelyn. Knowing my luck, I'll get some really awkward guy who will get mad at me because "I don't do any work." No one understands me better than Addie and Jocelyn. We finally get to school and go to our lockers that are all conveniently in a row. We start talking about Ricky who looks so cute today. Ricky and I dated for 11 months and I was so happy with him until one day he decides to dump me out of nowhere in front of the whole lunch room. How low is that? It just breaks my heart every time I see him especially when he looks so good in his football jacket and my favourite pair of jeans that I bought for him. I wonder what would happen if we got paired together for the science project. Science is last period so I am going to have to wait all day to find out my fate. The bells rings and Addie, Jocelyn, and I head to our first class.

We have all of the same classes, which is perfect to keep up on the weekly gossip. At lunch we sit at the same table every day. No one dares to sit there because it is ours.

When I say "ours" I mean all of the popular kids. The table is at the centre of the cafeteria so when Ricky broke up with me it was definitely public. Anyway, we talk about all of the latest gossip like the new girl who likes Ricky. That just isn't right. Who does she think she is? I can't deal with this. I have science soon and that is enough stress for me. Two bells and many bathroom talks later, it is finally time for science. The suspense is killing me. I have to know who my partner is because this is a long term commitment thing and if I get someone that I don't like, I don't think I can survive. I walk into class, arm in arm with Addie and Jocelyn. As soon as the teacher walks in I feel a rush of nervousness in my stomach. I start feeling little beads of sweat forming on my forehead. My palms start sweating. The bones in my hands start to shake. This never happens. Why is this happening? I try to control myself by looking at Ryan and Chris, two really cute guys in my class. "As you all know, you will be getting your lab partners for the semester long project today," said Mr. Rockenbach, our science teacher. Partner after partner, Mr. Rock just keeps reading off the list. Finally, my name is called. "Peyton and….

Here it is, the big moment! I must know! This is too much

stress!

“Peyton and Jeff!” Says Mr. Rock.

I automatically am relieved to know who my partner is, but that doesn’t mean I am happy with the choice. Jeff is a middle-class guy who is kind of quiet. He is pretty smart which is good for the sake of the project. But sometimes I just can’t deal with awkward. A major part of being popular is being social. We all sit next to our partners and wait for the assignment to come around. Now that I really look at Jeff, he is pretty cute. I guess I haven’t noticed this before because, well, I guess it is
because I have never really noticed Jeff before. Maybe this won’t be such a bad semester after all.
A few weeks into the project I was having a better feeling about everything. I started realizing that Jeff is a really sweet guy. He is so nice and really funny. He is one of the few people who I can actually have a real conversation with. I say “real conversation” as in talking about life and what happens in the world and not just gossip about other people. I know it has only been a few weeks but I kind of feel a little bad about myself. All Addie, Jocelyn, and I do is talk about other people. Whatever! We are still the most

popular girls in the grade!

One day after school, Jocelyn and Addie came over. I was lying on my comfy bed; Jocelyn was on the floor, lying on her stomach reading magazines, while Addie was checking herself out in the mirror. Jocelyn says, "Hey Peyton, how is your partner for the science project? He seems like a dork." When she said those words I felt this rage bubble up inside of me. I have no idea why this happened but I almost couldn't control myself.

"HE ISN'T A…", I nearly shouted. I paused took a deep breath and composed myself to say, "He is okay."

"But isn't he a dork?" asked Addie.

"Umm, yeah. I guess so," I said as I filled with guilt. I felt so bad about what I said. Even though no one besides Addie and Jocelyn were here but I still felt some guilt hang over me.

"I couldn't even imagine anyone who would want to date him, " laughed Jocelyn.

"He is so ugly. Like really c'mon! Who would want to kiss that?" chuckled Addie.

"Guys! Stop!" I said.

"Whoa! Peyton, calm down." Said Addie.

I felt so embarrassed. What if I actually like Jeff? I mean he is really sweet and I do think he is definitely a really good friend that I would like to have. But, dating?
On Thursday, we had a double period of science. This means an hour and a half of alone time for Jeff and me. I really wanted to take this time to get to know how I'm really feeling.
Jeff and I usually sit in the extra room across the hall. It is an abandoned classroom that isn't needed anymore. No one really uses it. Even though there are a stack of old chairs and desks, it is still a very peaceful environment. Jeff and I moved four desks in a cluster so that we have enough space to work. Another plus is that we can leave our work just the way we want. So we get to start right away and waste no time.
We get organized and head across the hall. Out of the corner of my eye, I can see Addie and Jocelyn whispering, giggling, and pointing at Jeff and me. They get Ricky to join in and I just keep walking like I didn't see anything. Deep down this really gets on my nerves. Ricky has no room to make fun of me after what he did, and Jeff is a

really good guy so I don't understand why they are being rude towards him. Do they know I might have feelings for him? I thought I was being very discrete. I don't look at him differently then I do any other guy. Do I? Maybe once I was staring at his cute dimples, but I promise that I caught myself right away. Like I said, I just ignore them and keep walking. As I close the door behind me, Jeff instantly starts a conversation. I sit in a chair and the entire time we are talking, laughing, and having fun while working on the project. The world around me seemed to vanish as if it were just Jeff and I on the planet. From the moment I stepped in the door, I swear I never stopped smiling.

Friday was an even better day. Jeff and I were in the middle of the project when we came to an awkward pause in the conversation. As I glance over, I see Jeff looking at me. He smiles and I can tell he was engulfed in embarrassment. At first I didn't understand why he felt this way, but after thinking about it deeply I think I understand. I realize that it must take a lot of confidence and guts to like a girl like me. I mean, like, I am the most popular girl in the school, and I do have a bit of a reputation of having high standards when it comes to guys. I know that if I was in Jeff's shoes I would be scared, and it would definitely take me some time to build up the confidence to even talk to someone like me.

I smile back, and we continue working on the project as I start a conversation. The bell rings about 10 minutes later. I am packing up my supplies and books when Jeff slides a piece of paper towards me on the desk. He walks out of the classroom with a smile on his face as I grab the note to open it. I look down and can't help but let out a little shriek. I am overwhelmed with joy as I smile from ear to ear. On the note Jeff had written down his phone number, name, and a dorky little smiley face. I got so much excitement out of one little piece of paper that deep down I think I might have some feelings for Jeff.

That night Jocelyn, Addie, and I are lying on my leather couch in my basement. The minute I got home from school I started texting Jeff. I couldn't help but get a little smirk on my face every time he texted me back. This is only a good thing when you're alone, but not with your best friends especially when they don't like him already.

"Who are you talking to?" asked Jocelyn.

"No one special," I replied.

Jocelyn gave me a sarcastic look because she knew I was lying.

"C'mon! Just tell us!" said Jocelyn.

"Seriously guys. It isn't important," I claimed.

"I am going to get it out of you sooner or later so you might as well tell us now."

"No I think I will pass."

"Peyton. We know you have standards so it's not like it is Jeff or someone low like him."

"Actually is it Jeff. And he isn't low! He is a really sweet guy and I can actually hold a conversation with him! Unlike some other people, not naming names."

"That hilarious! You actually give Jeff the time of day! And what do you mean you can actually have a conversation with him? That's what we do all the time."

"No we don't! All we ever talk about is other people! Jeff and I talk about life and what happens in the world like things that are actually important! So please just don't make fun of him."

"That's stupid. He isn't even popular."

"It doesn't matter! He is still a great guy whether he is rich, popular, or fits your opinion of someone I should date or not."

"Calm down! I was just saying. Whatever."

I never thought Jocelyn would treat me like this. This is

exactly why I don't want to tell them that I like Jeff, enough though they have gotten the idea.

Jeff and I had texted for a good week or two after he gave me his number, plus we have been working on the project for almost a month and a half now. We are really close friends, and I would definitely consider dating.

At school, Addie and Jocelyn gave me the cold shoulder for a while. I would still sit with them during lunch and all, but they seemed to be better friends while I was just the third wheel.

It was on a Tuesday when I came to a major decision in my life. Jeff and I were video chatting when he decided to tell me he has feeling for me. I was jumping out of my skin inside while telling him that I have feelings for him as well. He asked me out and there you have it, Jeff is now my boyfriend. The only issues are Addie and Jocelyn. I don't care what others think that much anymore because I like Jeff for who he is and he likes me just the same. But, I've seen those two in action before, and it can get pretty feisty. I already know now that when they find out they will think I am a joke. They will make fun and always have a nerve picking comment to make. That is just the way they are and as used to it as I am, it is VERY annoying.

The next day in school, Jeff meets me at my locker before

first period, which is science. As stereotypical as this sounds, he carried my textbook to class in one hand and I held the other. With a smile on my face and a good feeling inside, we walked to class together.

As soon as we walked into the door, all eyes are on us, especially Addie's and Jocelyn's. They both glared at me then looked at each other in disgust. Jeff saw this happen and shyly let my hand slip out of his. I could tell he was embarrassed. I grabbed his hand and held it tight. I wouldn't let them ruin my relationship. If that's how true friends act, then they aren't my true friends.

Again that week, Jeff and I were just about to kiss when Jocelyn made Ricky come up behind us and shove Jeff. I saw Addie and Jocelyn laughing hysterically. He banged into the lockers that we were leaning on and just stared down at his feet. I pushed Ricky back as he walked away laughing with Addie and Jocelyn. Ricky turned around, and I made sure he saw me kiss Jeff like I meant it. And boy did I! Ricky's faced turned red, and I knew he still felt something for me, which is most likely why he has been so rude. He really needs to get a taste of his own medicine, and I know that me dating Jeff is killing him inside.

My problem now isn't Jeff and me figuring out if I like him or not, it is Addie and Jocelyn. I thought they were my best friends. We have been through so much together. We have basically grown up together. Now after all of that, Jeff is the one who I know will always be there for me whether we are dating or not.

The year went on and Addie, Jocelyn, and I drifted apart. Jocelyn and Ricky dated for a few months until he broke her heart, just like he did to me. Addie and Jocelyn are the "most popular" girls in the school but I really could care less. Jeff and I are still going strong after almost a year now. We went to prom and spent spring break together with my new group of friends. I became close with three other girls named Lily, Ryan, and Bailey. We are like sisters now and we hang out all the time. We also hang out with Jeff and his closest friends Logan, Lucas, and Andrew. Dating Jeff has not only led to great things between us, but it has also really helped me find my true self. I learned that good friends, and in some cases those who are more than friends, are more important than a social status. I used to think that being popular was what life was all about, but as I look back to the person I was at the beginning of the school year, I couldn't believe that I was that girl. Yes, I still am my girly girl self with my fashionable clothes and my cute little dog, but on the inside I am more than that. I found true happiness throughout this year, and I can't wait to see what other stories the future brings for me. Going forward I will always remember: be your true self, have character, love endlessly, and always take chances because no matter what happens your true friends and the ones who really care will stick by your side the entire journey.

Alice, Baxter and David get out and Alice kicks the side of the car. The car makes a strange sound and the backdoor falls off a few inches. David notices a cute little posh tearoom in front of them, “I fancy some tea and cake.”

Alice smiles and nods, “So do I.”

Baxter makes a face, “And I fancy having a number two.”

Alice looks at Baxter with a stare, “You need the toilet again? You went four times already. What are you doing? Playing with yourself or something?”

Baxter goes bright red, “What if I have? It’s none of your business.”

Alice looks at Baxter blank faced, “So you have been playing with yourself.”

Baxter is about to answer when David cuts in, “I want tea and cake.”

They all walk into the posh tearoom.

Inside the very posh tearoom, the classical music "Clair de Lune from Suite Bergamasque' by Debussy plays quietly on a old- fashioned record player,

An old lady looks horrified when she sees the three misfits walking in and sitting at a table.

The old lady walks over to them and is about to say something when Alice speaks, "Three teas and three pieces of cakes please,"

All of the other people in the cafÉ are old ladies and gentlemen and look terrified at Alice and her friends.

The old lady smiles sweetly at them and whispers, "Could you three please leave? I don't want any trouble. We are about to close anyway."

David takes a bag of sugar from a little plate, rips it open and puts the condense of the sugar into his mouth then he moves on to another bag of sugar. Baxter looks up angrily at the old lady, "How can you be closing already? It's only 9:30 in the morning."

By now everybody in the tearoom is looking at they're table.

The old lady gives them a dirty look. It is clear that she doesn't like them one bit.

Alice takes out a cigarette, lights it up and blows smoke at the old cow, "We are not from London, you know."

David shakes his head and says sadly, "No we are from an even worst place, we are from Southampton, which is so shit rats even don't like to live there."

The old lady whispers to them in a horrible voice that sounds like what the wicked witch of the East sound like, "If your filthy people don't get out of my lovely tearoom I am going to call the police."

Baxter sighs and stands to leave, "Come on Alice, Dave we better go now. It's a crap place anyway."

Alice seems deep in thoughts for a moment and then speaks sweetly to the old lady, "Do you know my Lady DeMolay?"

The old lady looks shocked and surprised, "Miss May? She is your Auntie?"

Alice grins and then quite seriously says, "Yes and if you are whom I think you are then I think you should be nicer to us."

The old lady looks confused and snaps back at Alice, “And who do you thing I am?”

Alice whispers to the old lady, “The filthy dirty old lady that likes to videotape herself on camera with teenagers those are young enough to be your grandchildren.”

The old lady looks around in horror to make sure nobody is listening. Luckily for her nobody is, “You have no proof.”

With a sly smile Alice answers, “But I do. I found some old videotapes of my Auntie in a box this morning and you are the star of most of them. I was just wondering how do you get into those positions? Some of them look very painful,”

The old lady goes bright red and suddenly her manner changes. She smiles at the three of them, “Well why didn’t you say you are Lady DeMolay’ s niece?

You are more than welcome here. Please forgive me you have to be careful these days. You hear such awful stories. I was only joking anyway.

So what did you say you want? Some tea and cake?”

Baxter cuts in as he sat down again, “And four bottles of wine,”

David grins adding, “And three English breakfasts,”

Alice thinks for a moment and then says sweetly, "And desert afterwards."

The old lady smiles at them, "Of course, Anything else?"

Alice takes a puff of her cigarette and smiles back sweetly at the old lady before she answers, "Yes. You are going to let us have it all for free and you are then going to give us two boxes of your finest wine one red, one white when we leave, because I am the lovely niece of Lady DeMolay."

The old lady stares at them and gives them a shaky smile, realizing that she has no choice, and goes to get their (free) order.

Alice sits back, looking happy and relaxed, "What a lovely old lady she is,"

Alice, Baxter and David walk out of the posh tearoom carrying two large wooden cases which they put in the back of their car and they walk around window- shopping for a while until they come to an old- fashioned bookstore which they go into.

Inside they all choose a book each and take it to the counter where there is a plain looking middle- aged woman working behind the counter.

She adds up the prices for each book saying the titles of the book they have each bought.

The first being “Hard-core sex in the bedroom’ for Alice, the plain woman smiles at her and whispers, “” Hard-core sex in the bedroom’ Oh that’s a good one I read that one a few times myself, Try the position on page 75 when you have the chance, it’s like heaven,”

The next book is “How to control feelings for masturbation’ for Baxter. The plain woman looks at Baxter with a wink, “” How to control feelings for masturbation’ I like to do that myself from time to time,”

And finally we come to David’s book “The truth about worldwide conspiracies, aliens and everything else they don’t want you to know about’, “The truth about worldwide conspiracies, aliens and everything else they don’t want you to know about’ so it appears that we have a believer, “

She scans the book with a barcode reader , As David watches her in an uneasy way as if not trusting her one bit.

My mother keeps a jar of Loneliness in the cupboard: top right hand corner, next to the packet of Seething Resentment; both are past their sell by dates, both hardened and crystallized in the suffocating air. I beg her to throw them out, there are better things around now, I say, like that new Optimism that everybody is talking about; removes pessimistic stains and blemishes in only a couple of treatments, they say.

But no. She always says no. She simply hasn't the Wherewithal. But of course, she does. It's under the sink, next to the Gumption. If only she would use them again, like she once did; and I'm sure if she looked, she'd also find that gallon drum of Determination that she used to pour into everything — quite undiluted sometimes — until the place sang with it.

But not anymore. "How can I?" she would say, bitterly. "How can I after what your father did?" And I'd sigh. He couldn't help dying, of course, though she never quite saw it that way. I was there one day when a neighbour came around; left her a little sachet of Friendship, all bright and shiny and still warm from her touch. It came with suggestions: coffee mornings, theatre and help with the garden. My mother took the sachet, and thanked the neighbour politely, a rigours smile, and then put it on the bottom shelf. It has never been opened.

It's springtime, I tell her. Time to clean out that cupboard, and I open the door, picking up a tub of Boredom. She has stockpiled this for years, full strength — none of your polyunsaturated for my mother; this is saturated Boredom; Boredom that she spreads thickly around the house, working into cracks and crevices with a small trowel, a soft cloth and a rage that knows no bounds. I tell her it's not good for her. It will kill her in the end, I say. There are healthier substitutes now, like a good dose of Community Spirit, which people swear can work wonders.

But mother shakes her head and unscrews the lid of her deadliest weapon, the one that scrubbed and scoured our childhood, took the skin off our joy and killed all known dreams — dead. Martyrdom — passed on by her mother and her mother before her. I could smell its acidity, feel its corrosive properties. And, as ever, I cowered before it.

When I had my own children Mother reached into her cupboard and gave me a trial size of Emotional Blackmail. It came in a spray and smelt like misery, but had a lifetime guarantee, she said. I knew that only too well. I didn't want it. "No, Mother, no," I said. "Your cupboards are not my cupboards. My generation use different things, like Tolerance and Understanding… like Love." "Ah… Love." She laughed, grimly. "Now that really will kill you," and added, "When your generation become my generation then cupboards will be all you have left. Do you know that? Stock them while you can."

And so I take the offerings, pushing them to the back of my own shelf, where they ferment like rotten apples and blight the atmosphere. I should throw them out, I tell myself. I have no use for them. But then I spot a special offer, a two-for-the-price-of-one, and I can see the savings. So I put in an order. I probably won't even use them, there are other things that are better, like Resilience and Fortitude, but there's no harm in having them put by. No harm at all.

And, perhaps Mother is right: it's best to stock up while I can.

It's late around midnight and all three are sat on a sofa Alice and Baxter are watching an incredibly horrific horror film while David is reading his book about conspiracies with fascination and drinking beer, slowly David starts to drift off into a uneasy drug filled sleep, we close in on David's face as we embark on his very, very strange dream/nightmare,

We embark on a very surreal dream of David's starting with a,

, highly advanced high- tech satellite system in earth's orbit.

It makes a series of loud beeps and noises and then,

We are in a mysterious underground base like something from the X- Files,

People in military uniforms work around control panels and high- tech consoles,

One of the men in military uniform looks in amazement at his screen, "Oh my God, somebody's just bought it! You better notify him at once."

The white house,

We see a man in a dark suit rush down a corridor holding a print out. He rushes into the US Presidents room out of breath where the US President is sitting in Mickey Mouse boxer shorts on the floor watching the children's programme for under 10's "The Tweenies' sucking a lolly. He looks up angrily as the man rushes into the room and he snaps, "You better have a good reason for interrupting me. This is a good episode, this is where they make learn to cross the road,"

A man in a dark suit gently tells the President, "Mr. President, somebody has bought your book. We highly recommend that you deny any factor in this publication. We warned you this might happen. You shouldn't really have copied all those secret classified documents."

The President excitedly replies, "Are you telling me somebody has bought my book at long last?"

The man in a dark suit nods solemnly, "Yes, yes I am for God's sake. Do you know what this means?"

The President replies with joy, "Yes we should celebrate. I know what would happen if I press this big red button on my desk?"

In a panic the man in the dark suit screams, "Please God no! That's the button for the nuclear warheads.

Why don't you play your favourite CD and we will handle it from here,"?

The President sulks and looks at the red button on his desk, "Oh but I want to use it, I never get to use it,"

As if talking to a baby the man in suit goes down to his knee and smoothly says, "Now, now Mr. President calm down and play in your nice CD and we'll get you some ice-cream later."

The President claps his hands in joy, "Ice- cream wow, okay I'll put my CD in now,"

He picks up a big remote control and presses play. A disco-version of the "Tweenies- theme' starts to play throughout the room and says in amazement, "I just love this Erasure remix. Maybe Depeche Mode could do a remix of "YMCA' by the Village People. "

The man in dark suit smiles and walks behind him with a large injection and gives him the injection to make the President fall asleep, "I think we should wipe his brain again,"

Thinks for a moment

"If there was a brain to wipe,"

Thinks for a moment more,

"I hope that nobody in the human race finds out that everyone in power is really lizard being from the moons of Saturn,"

David wakes up screaming still holding his book, he looks up from the book he was reading before he had his strange dream and says with horror, amazement and wonder, “Do you know everybody in power in the worldwide governments are really lizard beings from the moons of Saturn,”

Alice and Baxter take no notice of what David is saying and Alice says instead, “How come that I have to watch another horror film?”

Baxter replies bored, “Because that’s the only thing the local TV stations seem to play here.”

Then they all hear a loud inhuman sound, which comes from outside the cottage. David looks up frightened spilling his beer, as do the others, “What was that?”

Baxter still bored yet a little frightened, “It could just be the wind.”

Then they all hear a scratching outside the kitchen door, David looks thoughtful for a moment while Baxter and Alice hug each other in fear, “They say the wind is the dead talking among themselves, in fact they say that out here in the middle of nowhere sometimes, the dead rise and come to look for the living, to eat humans brains so that they can taste life again, I think I once read that there was a cottage here in Wicker Point where friends were staying for a break and one night while they were watching a horror film. There was a loud sound outside the cottage, they thought it was only the wind,"

David breaks off speaking, Alice and Baxter stare at him, hitting themselves,

Alice jumps as they hear another loud moan come from behind the kitchen door, "Well what happened then David?"

David looks ahead if seeing hell before him and answers in a grave voice, "No one really knows for sure, only that they found them cut up in small, small bits, there was so much blood it was overflowing in the bath, they say it happen at Cottage 456, You know something I think I've just wet myself,"

Baxter cuts in with panic, "Fucking hell! This is cottage number 456,"

Now the sound is even louder it seems to come in the cottage. That's it they all had enough, they leap up from the sofa.

Alice says what they are all thinking, "Right, lets get all our stuff we're leaving."

They gather their belongings and rush out of the cottage. A moment later we hear their car start and they speed away leaving Wicker Point behind them.

There is a creepy sound about, almost inhuman, what could it be?

The door leading into the kitchen swings open quietly and a cute goat walks in, notices the spilled beer and starts to lick it up when a moment later David Bowie walks in and lets out a sigh of relief, “There you are china girl, I was beginning to worry about you. Come on let’s go home and get you some grass to eat.”

Thinks for moment

“In fact I will have some grass myself when I get home,”

With that they both leave the cottage.

CHAPTER 15

Alice and Baxter's car pulls up outside their home. They get the stuff from the boot and walk into their place looking tired and fed up.

Baxter lays out on the sofa sound asleep, exhausted from the trip back from Wicker Point.

Alice looks around for cigarettes and finds out that she is out of them. She calls up to David, "David can you be a dear and come down here when you finished using the loo?"

David is in the loo shooting up and it is clear that he is truly stoned. He calls back down to Alice in a dopey voice, "Be right down."

David walks into the living room straight into the coffee table. Alice giggles and looks at him fondly, "There will only ever be one David in Southampton. You have taken more drugs than Mick Jagger or the Oasis Brothers or all of them put together."

David starts to laugh out loudly like a lunacy psycho. Then he calms down and looks at Alice with a smile, "So what can I do for you Alice?"

Alice asks politely, “Could you be a dear and run down to the newsagent and get me some cigarettes? If you hang on for a moment I will get you some money,”

David cuts in gently and takes out a wallet full of cash there has to over a grand stuffed into it. Alice looks at him in amazement, “Don’t worry I will get you and Baxter as many cigarettes as you like.”

Alice looks puzzled at him, “David where did you get that money?”

David answers in a happy voice, “I took it from the till in that posh café when that old lady wasn’t looking.”

Alice laughs, “All right I thought you had done something serious for a moment. Okay I’ll have a cup of tea waiting for you when you get back from the shop. Be careful crossing that busy road and watch out for muggers.”

David nods and heads for the front door, “Okay I will, “

Sophie surveyed the menu in front of her.

Slow-roasted Prime Rib — Bet it wouldn’t be as prime as the gorgeous specimen sat opposite her. Sneaking a glance over the top of the menu, she drank in his delicious face: that immaculate hair falling over one of his brooding brown eyes, that nose that could have been carved straight from the face of a Grecian God, and oh, that chiselled jaw was just to die for. His eyes flicked up, and she hastily dropped hers back to the menu. If she wanted a second date, she would have to stop drooling all over him like a demented Labrador. Right, focus, food. The way her stomach was fluttering, it'd be a job to keep anything down. Perhaps a salad would be the safest option.

Classic Greek Salad — Could only be a let-down after having tasting it in the heart of the very country it was named for. Oh, what a summer that had been! Eighteen and carefree, she'd stepped off the plane feeling sure the next three months would be utterly blissful, and at first it had certainly seemed that way. Demetrious was everything she'd ever dreamed of in a man — suave, sophisticated, and sexy as hell. But it had all turned into a horrible cliché when she realised she was just this season's fling and had been forced to flee back to her parent's house in Shropshire to lick her wounds for the next two years. Yes, anything Greek was sure to be a disappointment.

She stole another glance at her date — except for that nose. She could make an exception for that.

Pan Fried Scallops — Although now she came to think of it, she was sure they had given her a nasty rash in a rather delicate area last time she'd eaten them. Her cheeks flushed as that awful memory suddenly swept over in full force. She'd been on a date with a lovely man she'd bumped into at her local library — a shy, scholarly chap, not her usual type at all. He'd taken her to a lovely little restaurant in the Quay and they'd had fresh scallops before she'd badgered him into coming back with her for "coffee". Things spiced up after she'd plied him with a few whiskies, but just as she ripped off her knickers he gasped in horror, stuttering something about having to water his plants, and ran out the door. She shuddered; scallops were definitely off the table.

Stuffed Oysters — Safe, perhaps. After all, they were supposed to be a natural aphrodisiac. On second thought, however, she didn't want to seem like she was coming on too strong. Coupled with the rather short skirt and push up bra she had picked out during a pre-date confidence crisis, oysters might give rather the wrong impression, and she was trying to get away from her past of saucy flings and one night stands. A steady relationship might finally stop her mother from harping on about the ticking of her biological clock and her distinct lack of forthcoming grandchildren. No, what she needed was a dish a little less provocative.

Risotto — Aha! What said “perfect girlfriend material” better than a nice risotto? Smoked haddock and spring onion, it sounded delicious. She hadn’t had a decent risotto since… oh, God. Since that night she’d ended up going home with a tattooed body builder who’d lasted about seventy-five seconds and then spent the rest of the night regaling her with tales of various contests, all of which he appeared to have lost, whilst his three dogs panted over her new boots. She’d finally managed to sneak out when he fell asleep around 5:00 and then had to endure the walk of shame before starting a ten-hour shift. She shuddered internally — perhaps not the risotto, then.

Pizza — Surely she couldn’t go wrong with a simple pizza. She could even suggest they share one. Or did that imply she was a little desperate to commit? If she ordered an entire pizza to herself though, he’d think she was a pig and after her last disastrous attempt at dieting, it was probably best she avoided too much stodge.

Nut roast — Innocuous enough, but then her last boyfriend had practically made her live off bloody nut roasts. A lactose-intolerant, gluten-free, vegetarian animal rights activist who liked to share one shower a week in order to preserve the planet's water and knit his own pants out of biodegradable wool. What on earth had she been thinking?

She was startled out of her ruminations as her date suddenly snapped his menu shut.

"I think I'll have the steak."

She breathed a sigh of relief. Steak! Of course! How could she have missed it?

"That's just what I was thinking, too," she said as the waitress approached, her eyes lighting up on catching sight of the delicious man in front of her. Her eyelashes instantly started to flutter as she took his order.

"What side would you like that with, *sir*?" she asked.

Sides! She hadn't noticed you had to pick a side. She scanned her menu furiously.

Chips — She'd seem common.

New Potatoes — Far too pretentious.

Sweet Potato Fries — Trying too hard.

She risked a glance upward and saw that her date was now appraising the waitress with rather more interest than she cared for.

The waitress finally turned to her, pen poised against her notepad.

Fuck it! "I'll have the oysters."

It's a bright sunny day in Southampton and David walks down the street high as a bomb, "What a lovely day. What could possibly go wrong?"

That's when a bird over him shits its load on him full in the face. Which in turn makes David walk into a lamppost, which makes him a little dazed and confused and he doesn't notice the black cat walking in front of him, so poor David falls over the cat and goes flying and hits his head on the pavement.

He gets up with a big cut on his forehead. He takes a step forward and steps on the foot of a huge powerfully built man who cries out in pain.

Before David can say "Sorry' the huge powerfully built man beats the crap out of him, leaving him a bloody mess. David gets up slowly and starts to walk off down the road when he comes across a cute- looking dog; Sitting waving its tail happily in the air and looking at David.

David smiles and pats the cute- looking dog on the head, That's when it attacks him; he leaps up and bites its teeth into David's manhood. David shakes around trying to dislodge the dog from his balls. After a good five minutes he manages to do so. The mutt lets out a happy bark raises his leg and pees all over David's shoes and then runs away.

David dazed and even more confused now and highly stoned wanders around in a daze and walks into a dustbin and notices a half- eaten burger next to it. He picks it up and starts to eat it as he starts to walk down the street.

We hear every sound he hears amplified very, very loudly,

Some schoolchildren walk by and yell something at him but he doesn't seem to notice. He is well and truly fucking stoned, he stops before he crosses the road.

On the other side is a newsagent. He looks up and down the road, Nothing, He steps out into the road and car misses him by inches. David says to himself, "That was lucky. I thought my time has come,"

That's when a bus hits him and kills him on the spot.

Two teenagers walk by notice the remains of David on the road and notice his wallet and pot lying beside him. They pick up the wallet and pot and walk off laughing and joking.

CHAPTER 16

It’s raining hard and the only people standing in the cemetery with Gabriel who is in his full priest clothes are Alice and Baxter.

They stand around David’s coffin while Gabriel says a few words.

Gabriel take out a large bottle of whiskey where he takes a sip from and passes it around.

David’s grave is yet to be filled with earth in the hole within the grave is loads of beer cans and cigarettes and a CD- Walkman.

Gabriel, Alice and Baxter each place a rose onto the coffin.

All three make the sign of a cross and Gabriel picks up a shovel and starts to fill the hole with earth.

Baxter nods over to Alice. She kneels down beside a portable stereo and hits play and we hear “Enjoy the silence’ by Depeche Mode playing loudly throughout the cemetery.

While “Enjoy the silence’ is playing at the cemetery Alice and Baxter say their last respects, “David’s death came as a shock to all of us and he will be missed.”

They suddenly realized that they weren’t clever or big for taking drugs so much so that they came to an agreement,

They wouldn’t take anymore-hard drugs ever. I think it took something very tragic to happen in your life to make you realize how fragile life really is,

Baxter flushes down all the hard drugs that he and Alice have down the toilet.

Baxter cries as he does this, “I’m so sorry David I should have been a better friend. I should have tried to help you quit when I saw your arms at that time with all those needle marks,

Some fucking family we were to you. No harder drugs no more I promise on your soul.”

Alice stands in the doorway watching him with tears in her eyes. She goes over quietly and stands behind Baxter and for a moment it appears that she is going to reach out and hold him but she seems uncomfortable being there as if she would interrupt Baxter during something important.

She changes her mind and walks quietly out of the bathroom.

Baxter doesn't even realize that she was there with him and carries on crying the tears of someone who has lost a close friend,

CHAPTER 17

Gabriel is in a busy gay nightclub and for some strange reason he is still wearing his priest clothes. Before him are a round about six empty pint glasses on his table.

A loud disco number starts to play on the speakers. Gabriel downs his pint and rushes to the dance floor and starts to do a dance number that John Travolta would be proud of.

The track suddenly becomes a song called "World (The Price of Love' by New Order and Gabriel loves it. He takes off his black jacket and does a complex break dance routine. The crowd go wild and cheer and yell as another 90's pop song called "No Limit' starts to play,

Two gay clubbers look on they are both dressed in white vests and tight black leather trousers, and speak to each other, "They are playing a lot of disco tonight,"

Another gay gentleman watches as Gabriel wiggles his bum to the crowd and answers his friend, "Well, I'd rather have 90's dance tracks than Take That, they make us gays look even gayer than we are,"

His friend takes a sip of his pint and nods agreeing.

After a while Gabriel has enough and returns to his table where a waitress comes over and speaks excitingly to him, “Hey listen Gab I have a brother who I would love you to meet. He is a truck driver. He’ll be here in 15 minutes. He’ll give you a lift back home later if you like?”

Gabriel finishes his drink and gives a loud burp and smiles at the waitress, “Sure sweetheart. I could say hi, I could do with some company anyway.”

Later on in a truck. There is a strong looking man, handsome in a rough sort of way.

Gabriel sits next to him, humming to the tune “The Truck and His Mate’ by the Pet Shop Boys.

Gabriel pats his hand on the knee of the truck driver and says, “Oh by the way when you stay over tonight we have to be quiet as I have my sister and her friend staying over as well.”

The truck driver smiles back fondly at Gabriel and turn the music even louder before he answers, “Fine by me. By the way you look great in black.”

Gabriel laughs and the truck drives off into the moonlight.

Alice and Baxter are fast asleep in the middle of Gabriel's living room. Cans of beer and left over pizza are on the floor around them.

The time on the video player reads 2 am. Gabriel and the truck driver walk in and quietly step over Alice and Baxter and tiptoe up the stairs quietly.

Baxter wakes up and gets muttering to himself, "God I need a loo,"

He passes the video player where the time now reads 2:45 a.m. and heads over to the stairs and goes up them.

He notices a door and walks towards it.

Baxter walks into the bedroom not realizing that it is Gabriel's room and turns on the light and stops dead in his tracks as he sees Gabriel holding the truck driver in his arms.

Baxter looks at Gabriel, Gabriel looks at Baxter. The truck driver looks at Gabriel and Baxter.

For a moment they all look embarrassed.

Baxter speaks quietly, "So okay Gabriel I understand. Everybody needs somebody,"

Gabriel looks at Baxter in an almost ashamed way, "Please don't tell Alice. She wouldn't understand,"

Baxter smiles fondly at Gabriel, "It's okay. We will keep this our secret old friend."

Gabriel smiles fondly at his friend.

The truck driver leans over to the bedside cabinet and takes a cigarette lights it and watches Gabriel and Baxter, "Thanks. I always knew you are the right one for my sister."

Baxter winks at the two lovers. He goes to leave the room. Before he does so he turns around, "Good night Ladies, see you in the morning."

He leaves the room as the two-lover laugh as he closes the door.

Alice and Baxter sound asleep snoring loudly.

The truck driver comes down the stairs, steps over them and leaves. The door closes behind him quietly.

Gabriel comes downstairs with a big smile on his face, looks around at the mess on the floor and picks up a can of beer.

He opens it and tales a mouthful and looks for a moment as if he is about to be sick but he manages to hold it down. He takes out a cigarette lights it with his silver lighter and starts to smoke.

It is clear from the movements behind Alice's eyelids that she is dreaming,

Dark clouds hover over Alice's dream landscape. We are in the middle of Southampton precinct the place is eerily deserted there is no one around apart from Alice who stands very still.

The haunting music called "Out of the blue' by Moby begins to play,

A blast of wind blows around her. She stares at the Southampton landmark the Bargate, which suddenly radiates out light that's when the water starts to flow around the precinct. Suddenly the whole of Southampton is submerged in water with a galactic water tide. Just the top the buildings can be seen.

Alice doesn't seem to care and starts to swim; an expression of joy on her face.

Dolphins appear; they jump around her. Alice takes the fin of one of them and she sails along with it. The dolphins make sounds of joy.

Suddenly the dark clouds open to let rays of brilliant sunshine that shines it's light upon the blue water.

Magnificent winged angels fly down within the light. There is something almost biblical about this image. One of the angels flies down and takes hold of Alice's hand. Alice takes hold and she is lifted into the beautiful blue sky.

Suddenly the blue sky turns into a night sky full of brilliant and beautiful white stars. In the distance Alice can see solar systems, planets and the most beautiful, amazing and wonderful objects that she has ever seen.

She notices two angels hold each other within this wonderful place and kiss.

They seem to sense Alice looking at them. They smile and one of them points downwards. Alice follows where the angel is pointing to and sees Baxter lying on the floor in Gabriel's house. He is sleeping. There is something almost child- like by the way he sleeps.

Alice smiles and speaks to the angels, "I understand, I think it is time I told him. I waited long enough,"

Suddenly Alice is engulfed brilliant unearthly white light.

Alice slowly opens her eyes,

Baxter wakes up at the same time and sits up coughing. He picks up a bottle of whiskey and starts to drink.

He notices Alice staring at him intensely, “Okay Alice, are you all right?”

Alice smiles, “More than all right; I think I have been touched with the hand of God.”

Baxter puzzled as usual in the morning, “What? Like the New Order song?”

Alice grins, “Yeah just like that. Listen I have something to tell you. Something important. Something I should have told you years ago. I love you Baxter and I always have,”

Baxter stares at her for a moment and bursts out laughing, “That’s a good one. I thought you would have been serious for a moment.”

Alice stares at him in a shock, going red, “But it’s true I always have loved you.”

Baxter laughs even harder, “Please stop I don’t wanna die laughing. This is so funny,”

Alice looks as if she is about to cry but Baxter doesn't seem to notice, "You don't feel the same way? Are you gonna tell me everything we have ever done, every hit and miss moment in our life was unrequited?"

Baxter stops laughing and for the first time seems to realize what Alice is saying, "I never knew you felt that way. I mean I knew we are very close friends and I know you do anything for me but I need some time here. I just can't say that I love you like that. I need some time,"

Alice can't believe what she just heard and suddenly busts into tears.

Baxter looks embarrassed and does what he would normally do. He offers her a drink from the bottle of whiskey he is holding.

Alice not believing what she is seeing or heard slaps him hard across the face and drops the bottle out of Baxter's hand.

She goes mad smashing all the drinks in the drinks cabinet and kicks Baxter between the legs with her knee.

Baxter lets out a high-pitched scream like a girl and falls on the ground holding his manhood.

Alice looks down regretting what she just has done and starts to cry even more and runs out of the living room.

A moment later we hear the front door slam shut behind her. Gabriel finishes drinking his can and watches Baxter for a moment, unsure what to do.

And then gently says, “Go and tell her how you feel Baxter. Don’t let her be a victim of a hit and miss on unrequited love. Tell her how you feel. You are both made for each other.”

With that Gabriel vomits and falls asleep.

Baxter takes a quick drink out of Gabriel’s can and goes after Alice.

Alice is stood leaning over the wall edge of the bridge starring off into the distance as if looking for an answer to her problems.

Somewhere the ballad “To The End’ by the group Blur starts to play, making the scene even more romantic,

Her fair hair blown gently in the wind, Baxter watches her with affection for a while.

He walks over to her and Alice looks around surprised to see him.

Without a word he takes her into his arm and for a moment just holds her.

They remain embraced silhouette in the moonlight.

Epilogue

Aka the ultimate psychedelic trip of the end of the beginning of Alice and Baxter.

I saw him again, the strange man in the white suit. He stood a little way away smiling, that's when it happened, the most wonderful strange thing to ever happen to anyone. The stars above seem to glow with unholy light.

Brighter and brighter still. They fell around us. We both bathed in the light. The light of stars swirled and seemed to form a vortex what could only be called some sort of tunnel which seemed to go on forever and ever. The stars sped past us, faster and faster, my god even faster. Worlds were born, destroyed, new worlds become eyes. They watched us for years and years. Until the years became million upon each other, and still we went so fast. Holding each other, worlds that I knew had life on them cheered with delight as we went past them.

Then suddenly we were in a room that overlooked Southampton high street but we both knew it wasn't real. For starters the sky was red, the streets empty.

The room was white. Bright white, the walls suddenly have colours, they swelled and changed, opening the wall. An ancient David, old and wrinkled, reading Halloweenies, by JAD Blackmore, eating his meal, he took no notice of us.

A portrait of Gabriel comes to live and smiles down on them.

A child's bike rolled past us. IT reminded me of a bike I had as a child but it melted away.

The walls of the room turned to dust. In the distance a mushroom cloud appeared. It was then that it started to rain, that was when we became aware that we didn't have any forms, no bodies. We were angry, a state of weariness that could perhaps be what could be called souls.

A faceless person appeared. We stared at the person but got bored.

True Faith played in the background somewhere.

Moving plants, we moved at an incredible speed with our minds, but even that gets boring after a while... millions of years...

We waited and waited until we saw earth in its wondrous glory. Our old home. It was nice to see it again. Like an old friend that you haven't seen in years.

It became clear.
We knew it was a second chance that many people don't get. The light of the sun bathed us. We held each other as we took shape. A heart beat could be heard. Water filled our figures. Baxter was gone but I knew in time I would see him again. I saw light and doctors and nurses staring at me. I let out a cry… I was home.

A small boy that bears a remarkable resemblance plays outside Auntie Mo' s cottage which now looks absolutely beautiful with a new painting job, new windows and doors and is surrounded by all manner of lovely flowers.

A small fair- haired girl at the same age as the boy, that looks like Baxter, rides up on a bike. The boy smiles and takes out packet of sweets and offers one to the girl.

It is clear they two know each other; by the way they laugh and giggle together.
She takes a sweet from the boy and pops it into her mouth.

For a moment they stare at each other fondly and suddenly the little girl leans over and kisses the little boy on the cheek.

The little boy pushes her away embarrassed and laughs. The little girl looks upset and walks away pushing her bike aside her.

The little boy chases after her and starts to walk beside her.

After a moment he reaches out and takes her hand in his hand and they both walk off giggling like only children can when they are happy. The boy and girl walk away holding his new friends hand.

The sun starts to set over the cottage and we hear the song 'More than this' by the Cure from somewhere.

18486273R00122

Printed in Great Britain
by Amazon